THE
MISADVENTURES
OF
HECTOR MACLEOD

THE MISADVENTURES OF HECTOR MACLEOD

OF

IN THE GEORGIAN BAY
AND THE
LA CLOCHE DISTRICTS

HUGH COWAN

THE MISADVENTURES OF HECTOR MACLEOD – In the Georgian Bay and La Cloche Districts

Copyright © 1928 by HUGH COWAN.

Published By: Silverwoods Publishing—a division of McK Consulting Inc.

Cover photo by Scott M. Fairley

Toronto ~ Windsor ~ Chicago

ISBN: 978-1-897202-28-9

Originally Entitled

LA CLOCHE

THE STORY OF HECTOR MACLEOD AND HIS MISADVENTURES IN
THE GEORGIAN BAY AND THE LA CLOCHE DISTRICTS

First Published under the Auspices of the

ALGONQUIN HISTORICAL SOCIETY OF CANADA

REV. HUGH COWAN, M.A., BD.

Managing Editor

INTRODUCTION

This adventure tale was the creation of my great-grandfather, Hugh Cowan (1867-1943) and was published in 1928. His journey included life as a minister, historian, editor and an author. More about his story is included at the end of this book. As editor of *Mer Douce**, the publication about the Georgian Bay area, he also wrote fiction targeted at young readers along with the articles on history, theology and current events.

Beyond just the pleasure of reading this book, I was enchanted by some of the pieces of family history discovered and experienced. In the winter of 2013, an expedition with my cousin Nancy's husband, Greg De Souza, took us into the area of Owen Sound area where Cowans had farmed and lived before moving to Manitoulin Island. It was also the community where many of the Cowans who eventually left the island chose for their retirement years including Hugh. Canadian genealogist Janet Isles of Owen Sound was very helpful in the quest. We were delighted to meet Joan Hyslop at the Grey Roots Museum and Archives. It turns out that she too was another descendant of Hugh's parents, John and Mary Cowan who came to Canada from Scotland.

Encouraged by our progress, I took a trip with my son Scott in the summer of 2013. It was our first visit to Manitoulin Island and the western side of Georgian Bay. There we enjoyed the company of many people who helped us begin the exploration of some of the Cowan history that still can be found there. Local Manitoulin historians Derek Russel and Doug Tracy were very helpful. We also visited the Assiginack

Museum in Manitowaning where the curator, Jeanette Allen shared a number of records and photographs with us from the early years of the Cowans in Canada there.

We learned how much of a challenging existence the family faced to farm and survive in the wilderness of late 1800s in Tehkummah and Assiginack townships of Manitoulin Island. We also began to understand the wonder of this rugged and beautiful place that had captured the imagination of artists like those of the Group of Seven, photographers, cottagers and tourist for generations.

As copies of this book were rare, we wanted to once again share his imagination with new readers who, like the author, may have a special love of the rugged beauty of Georgian Bay, Manitoulin Island and the La Cloche district of Ontario, Canada. Manitoulin Island is the world's largest freshwater island, surrounded by Lake Huron on one side and Georgian Bay on the other. It was where Hugh and his siblings grew up. It was a region where he returned to vacation and to live during different chapters of his life. The setting includes a historian's care to present the context and the images of a bygone era. Let the adventure (or more correctly—the misadventures) come to life again!

Mer Douce meaning "sweet sea" was a nickname of Georgian Bay.

Grant D. Fairley
February 2014

ACKNOWLEDGEMENTS

My beloved wife, Cari patiently endures my need to know more about our family history. In fact, she too has been infected with the ancestry bug and also enjoys exploring the McKenzie and other roots of her family tree. The next generation is variously puzzled and amused by our desire to know more about our ancestors. They kindly tolerate my journeys into the mists of the past. While I assure them since I am alive that I am not yet an ancestor myself, they may correctly conclude that this is a distinction without a difference in my case.

Thanks to each of the family members who have encouraged our connection with those Cowans and others who went before us. Special appreciation goes to Jennifer Alvarez for the patient and thorough transcription of the original copy of the book. The book formatting was the work of wonderfully arranged by Jeny Lyn Ruelo. The cover design was by my wife, Cari Fairley.

This project would not be possible without the people who preserved their physical copy of this book as it was published in 1928 in an age before digitization, the internet and cloud servers.

PREFACE

Librarians, seeking the class of literature to which this narrative belongs will perhaps list it under the title Fiction. Historians, acquainted with the immediate past and its peoples may be tempted to designate it Biography. The writer is indifferent in respect to what class of literature it belongs, If only the constructive imagination of the reader is stimulated to see a true likeness of conditions as they existed in the Lake Region just one short century ago.

The Bible pictures life as it ought to be; literature pictures it as it might be; history portrays it as it was and is. This narrative is a portrayal of life as it was, but no longer is, nor will ever again be. The old order has passed out; the new has taken its place; for we are born to progress and advance not to stagnation and retrogression.

CONTENTS

CHAPTER I

HECTOR CAMPBELL MACLEOD

"You'll be wanting to see the islands, Hector, I'll be thinking."

The speaker was an aged sea-captain who had already left fourscore years behind him, more than half of which he had spent upon the Mer Douce and the other great inland hikes which separate the United States from Canada. His remarks were addressed to a young collegian, his grandson, Hector Campbell MacLeod, who, with three others of his chums, were making preparations to take a summer vacation on one of the Thirty Thousand Islands of the Georgian Bay, the forerunners of that procession of tourists from the cities of southern Canada and America who now spend the July and August of their summers on one of these places of healthful resort.

"Yes, Grandfather, we are going next week and we hope to stay until the deer season begins, if we can manage it," the grandson answered with cheerful hope.

"It's myself that would like to see you go to La Cloche, but you'll not be wanting to go so far north."

"The arrangements are for a camp on one of the islands near the middle east shore, Grandfather."

"Ay, ay, that would be far enough. Did your father say who would go with you?"

"Arrangements have been made with a trader by the name of Rusty Brown, who will prepare us a camp and look after us while we are there."

Hector spoke in a clear tone of voice, slowly uttering each word that his grandfather might not miss anything of the sentences or their meaning, for fourscore years had dulled somewhat the acuteness of his hearing.

"Would you like us to go to the La Cloche instead, Grandfather?" he continued.

"It's not myself that would be asking you to go to the La Cloche, if your father has said the islands. And what for does he want you to go to the islands?"

"There'll be splendid fishing in the island channels, he says, and we may be able to get some deer on the near mainland."

"Ay, there'll be deer at the La Cloche at any rate, but I'm not after being so sure there'll be deer near the islands."

After this remark the grandfather lapsed into silence, adding no further word concerning their proposed outing. A man above the average in weight and height, unstooped in shoulder notwithstanding his age, his was still a striking figure. He wore a long beard, now pure white, which extended far down his breast, and of which he gave daily evidence that he was justly proud. His hair, white as his beard, hung in disordered curls around his head and neck. His face was angular, but pleasant looking and with deep brown eyes, gave appearance of once being handsome. The grandson was not wanting in characteristics strikingly similar to this paternal ancestor of their family.

"Why did you say the La Cloche?" Hector asked, after a considerable period of silence.

"I'll be after telling you, Hector, seeing it is your own namesake. It was there that the Injun saw Hector Campbell last."

"Father's uncle; your youngest brother?"

"Ay, and the Injun said he was in the whiskey business. Poor Hector!"

"I suppose it is he I'm called after."

"You are called after your father, and your father is called after him, but it was on the mother's side of the house the Hectors have come down to us. There hasn't been a generation of the Campbells without a Hector.

Poor Hector!" he repeated, and the grandson saw a deepening moisture overshadowing the old man's eyes.

"But how did you get parted from him?"

"He went to Ameriky and the war, and it was the Hessians that made him desert. The Germans, I am thinking, have come down to us through the ages from Judas and his family. There was some shooting in the army and Hector got mixed up in it. Och, hone!"

"Was Uncle Hector a good shot?" the grand-nephew asked, his interest at once aroused in this branch of sportsmanship in which himself excelled.

"Ay, ay, that's what for he became the Lieutenant."

"Father says it was from him I get the gift."

"It's no gift, Hector, and if you've got it, don't be too ready with your gun. The MacLeods were always too ready with their guns and their fists."

Hector laughed as he observed the animated spirit with which his grandfather couched his reproof and warning.

"I'll take care, but I would like to have a line on a deer or a moose all the same before I go back to college this fall."

"I was the same when I was young, but I'm not staying long here now, Hector, and if you are around the La Cloche, you might keep your ears open, if there is any person the name of MacLeod, it might be my brother Hector."

The disclosing of this piece of information gave to the grandson an added interest in that great area of wilderness stretching northward from the great lakes to Hudson's Bay. The deer, grazed in its beaver meadows and the moose found food and shelter among its underwoods, but of more importance to him now was the fact that somewhere in its recesses there was living or buried a scion of his own race.

CHAPTER II

FLORA MACLEAN

The story of how and why Hector MacLeod became lost to his family is easily and soon told. The Revolutionary War was at its height when he and his cousin Rory MacKenzie enlisted as privates in a Highland Regiment, just then being detailed for overseas service in America.

This, Lieutenant Hector MacLeod deemed a fortunate circumstance in his career. There he would meet with Flora. MacLean, his espoused, and the day of their marital vows would not be long delayed after he set his foot on her father's threshold in that new and now their adopted land. He had grown up with her from childhood, on their native heath in Scotland, and oftentimes rambled together among its hills and dales and picturesque locks as playmates, she becoming more. And more a part of his mind and heart until the day came when they had to be parted, he for the army, and she, with her family, to that land so rich in promise—America.

When her family left Scotland, she was not much more than a girl, sixteen, and he but two years her senior; yet their attachment to each other was as enduring as it was sincere. But their parting, through the fortuitous circumstance of the Revolutionary war, was of only a few short years of duration. When they met again, the last link which joined them together as one was welded by the chaplain of the army. One more turn of the wheel of destiny was all that was now needed—the ending of this fratricidal carnage of blood, the disbandment of the soldiery, and the even current of their lives would then run smoothly on to the end. Already a friend had chosen for him his allotment of land in the Detroit district and he only awaited the hopeful day of his discharge, when he would take possession of this grant, and enter into that era of happiness which his hope had Visualized before him.

Fate, however, decreed otherwise for Hector Campbell MacLeod. His cousin, Rory, now promoted to Captain, was attached to another unit from Hector's, a battalion which, on one occasion, was stationed at "The Beeches," the name of Colonel MacLean's villa. Colonel MacLean was a Loyalist, and this gave the British Regiment liberties with his place and property which would not have been taken with that of a Revolutionist. Rory MacKenzie had heard of Flora MacLean and knew of his cousin's marriage, yet he had not associated this villa with that of his cousin's family home, until after they had been stationed there a. few hours. A subaltern entered his quarters, with a. message which occasioned him no little surprise.

"The young lady of the house wishes an audience with Captain MacKenzie this afternoon at three o'clock."

Captain MacKenzie could not conjecture why he should be asked to have an audience with one concerning whose identity he was as yet completely ignorant.

"Who lives there?" he asked rather abruptly, as soon as the message had been delivered.

"At The Beeches, sir?"

"Yes,"

"Colonel Farquhar MacLean, sir; a Loyalist, sir."

"Oh!" he exclaimed, now quite enlightened. "You may inform the lady that I shall not fail to keep the appointment."

The subaltern went forth to deliver his message, and Captain MacKenzie followed to the door of his tent, and cast his eyes observantly over the villa. Numerous cattle and horses were grazing on its pasture-lands; an abundant harvest of corn stood in shocks out on the fields, for it was September; servants were seated in groups, husking; others were drawing the husked cobs to the cribs.

"Farquhar MacLean has certainly prospered in this new world if all this is his own," he remarked to himself as he saw the evidences of prosperity all around him. "Flora, Hector's bride," he quietly soliloquised, as he thought over the message he had received.

At the hour appointed, he duly presented himself at the gate and was soon ushered in to the big living room which comprised the centre of the house—or series of houses erected side by side which went under the name of "The Beeches." Several officers of the Hessian troop were seated round, lounging and smoking as their manner was. The servant, who ushered him in, led him out through a back door and brought him round to the south door of the house. As soon as he stepped on the porch floor, the door opened and a young woman of gentle beauty greeted him.

"You are Captain MacKenzie, are you not?"

"I am, and at your service. Hector's Flora, I presume?"

"I am so glad your battalion has arrived," she said, as she took him by the hand and ushered him in. "I sent for you because you are my husband's cousin, and we are in need of counsel and protection, since my father and brother, as well as my husband, are all at the war."

Again Captain MacKenzie assured her he was entirely at her command.

"You know that the Hessian officers are quartered at our home," she began with some hesitation.

Rory nodded assent.

"Twice, one of these entered into my apartments unbidden. I informed him on both occasions that his visits were unacceptable and that he must not repeat them."

"Surely he wouldn't refuse to respect your wishes, and do violence to the hospitality which your father has so generously shown them," interrupted Captain MacKenzie, with evident disgust and anger.

"He came yet a third time and I could not get him to leave until I had called in the servants."

"But,—but,—" Rory stumbled and stuttered, and could hardly find words to frame the sentence he fain would express. "He knows you are married. What can be his motive?"

Flora blushed deeply and her whole countenance was overcast with shame as in great agitation and with trembling voice she answered his question.

"When I think of that I am mortified and angered that those whom our loyalty compels us to treat with hospitality and respect should regard us on the same plane, in relation to culture and virtue, as themselves."

At this stage in the conversation, the door opened gently and Flora's mother came stealthily into the room. She threw her gaze from one side to the other and then went out as she came in.

"Poor mother!" Flora's eyes filled with tears as she spoke, "She is acting so queerly these days. I am afraid her mind is being unhinged."

"These men have no right making their quarters here, with your father and brother in the war. I shall see to it that they leave at once today."

"Do you think are we not safe?" she asked with increased agitation and concern.

"In this country, with hired criminals quartering themselves upon you without leave or authority from anyone, a young woman of your youth and beauty, Flora, is safe only where the protection of the Unseen God makes it safe. These men do not believe in either virtue or God and they will surely act in accordance with their unbelief. Keep you your mother and your maid always by your side as long as they remain in your home. Two or three women of virtue together may be safe with these Hessians around; one alone, never. This is war, Flora, and many crimes are committed to-day in the name of war."

"Oh, I know what you say is true, but God grant that it may be soon over."

Just then the bugle-call for muster was sounded.

As Captain MacKenzie hastily arose to respond, he unbuckled his pistol, and laid it on the bureau.

"There, Flora, I am leaving you that. Keep it near you. You may need it."

"But I have never shot a gun off in my life, Captain."

"Then keep someone near you who has. You cannot afford to take any chances with drunken Germans."

"But they are Loy—, I mean they are on our side."

Captain MacKenzie shrugged his shoulders.

"The soldier who would insult a fellow-soldier's wife in her own home is on no side, Flora, except the side of selfish wrong and crime. The service which may require the sacrifice of life, cannot be hired for so many English pounds sterling. If you will take the advice of a friend, keep the door between you and everyone of them bolted, unless you have Hector by your side, or a mastiff lying at your feet. I shall see to it that they shall leave these quarters at once."

Captain MacKenzie spoke with emphasis, but he reckoned without his host, if he deemed he had either sufficient authority or influence to carry out his purpose to rid the Villa Beeches of the Hessian officers. At any rate the occasion for exercising that influence was not to present itself. In war, as in all the events of our life, circumstance determines Occasion, and these flit by too swiftly to enable us to seize and profit by them. Thus it was in this instance. When Captain MacKenzie's interview with his cousin's bride was brought to an abrupt close by the imperative of this bugle call, it was because a contingent of the army of the revolutionary colonists were marching forward to give battle to the King's forces stationed at The Beeches.

Captain MacKenzie met the enemy, not in defence, but attack. His mind and body were keyed for super-human alertness. Attack followed attack, wisely led and increasingly effective. The Revolutionists wavered, gave way and withdrew to the opposite side of the hill, yet not without some measure of success; a few of the Loyalist men were wounded; one was killed and several taken prisoners. Among them was Captain MacKenzie, who had taken no precaution to keep himself from exposure. Slightly wounded, he fell into their hands, only to make his escape in a few short days after. Had this casualty not taken place, the story which we are seeking to chronicle would not have been written.

When the battle was over, both armies moved out of the neighbourhood. The villa of MacLean was once more to enjoy the pleasure of its liberty. To none more than to Flora was the going away of the Hessian staff a pleasure. For the first time since their arrival she was able to move about, her mind freed from the restraint, the fear and the forebodings which their presence produced. She breathed freely as she saw the last of them pass over the hill out of sight, followed by their soldiery. But he laughs best who laughs last. Flora's pleasure was destined to have a rude and abrupt ending.

It was only a short hour after their departure, when a rider on horseback came up the lane, dismounted, tied his horse, and went round to the south door, the one opening into the apartments of Flora. Without kicking, the door being unlocked, he opened it and walked in. It was Oscar Rheinhardt, the Hessian officer. The sight of him had the same effect upon her that an apparition of the night might be expected to have on one suddenly awakened. The soul of purest virtue in the presence and alone of a foul and uncultured criminal. Flora MacLeod stood paralyzed by the suddenness of the apparition.

There was another, however, who saw the rider come up the lane, saw his shadow pass her window, heard the door open and his salutation. It was Flora's mother. Stealthily she crept into the room and reaching out took possession of MacKenzie's gun. She pointed it at the intruder and discharged. A movement of his head saved his life. The bullet passed through one cheek and came out on the opposite side through the other.

She cocked the second hammer, placed her finger on the trigger, made steady her aim, for she was determined to make a successful achievement of her self-imposed task. Rheinhardt leaped, the blood running profusely from his face, and grasped the hand of his assailant, to deflect her aim. In the conflict the barrel was discharged; Rheinhardt escaped, but the bullet passed into the body of Flora MacLeod and killed her almost instantly.

While this tragedy was being staged at The Beeches, the unit of Lieutenant Hector MacLeod kept bravely fighting on its losing battles against the Revolutionists. No respite seemed to be forthcoming from the constant strain and weariness of the war. A day, however, came when the staff consented to a fortnight's leave of absence. Lieutenant MacLeod exulted with boyish glee as he mounted the steed that was to bring him to the home which sheltered the one which was dearer to him than life itself.

When he neared The Beeches, he stayed his horse, and paused for a moment while memory gleaned in the field of bye-gone days, and he saw once more in vision the young girl of his youthful hopes, her face to him always beautiful because the index of a beautiful soul—so sweet, so gentle, and in her fidelity to virtue so strong—the heart which never knew evil passion, and the will which could not be made a party to deception and guile. In a few minutes he would hear once more the sound of her voice and the ring of her merry laughter.

As he looked up and cast his eyes over the villa, he was surprised and impressed with its and deserted appearance. Where the workmen, the cattle and the grain fields? All at once the truth dawned on him. This home had been changed by this Civil War into a desert. Everywhere about were the sure evidences of a battlefield, with the woods on the banks of the stream for the cover of one of the belligerents, and the valley beyond the hill as the rendezvous of the other. The house was intact as were all the buildings, but the fences were demolished and about the yard the litter of a soldier's encampment.

The young cavalry officer leaped from his horse, tied it to a hitchpost, once so familiar and almost running, hastened to the door and knocked. There was no answer. He knocked still more loudly. Still no answer. He moved about crest-fallen. Had they been taken prisoners? No. Civilians would not be taken prisoners. He looked towards the barn and saw a man observing him from within the stable through the aperture of a slightly opened door.

Waving his hand for him to come forward, he was rewarded by seeing the man emerge from his place of concealment and come towards him.

"What has happened here and where are the folks?" he asked imperiously.

"A fight in the woods, there, sir and—"

"Yes, yes, I know, but where are the folks?" he interjected impatiently.

"Folks, sir? You mean Colonel MacLean?"

"Yes, yes, and his family. Where are they?"

"The old woman's in the house somewhere—all that's left of them now, you know, and she's—" and he tapped his head to indicate that an aberration had taken place there. "Can't you let me in?"

"I'll see; but it's not easy getting in there any more, especially for strangers—and wearing your clothes," he added, as he saw him dressed in soldier's garb.

The old man entered by way of a back door which he immediately locked after him. After what seemed to the Lieutenant an interminably long time, he came back the same way he went in, again locking the door after him.

"Be you Lieutenant MacLeod?" he asked.

"Yes, yes, but why do you ask?"

"If you be Lieutenant MacLeod, go round to the south door and I'll let you in, sir."

The young man stalked hastily to the door he knew so well, and waited impatiently the arrival of the man, who apparently was only caretaker which this once busy villa now knew.

Quicker than expected, the door was opened, and he was led to the well-known room with its large fire-place, and sacred with the memories of the young girl which here he had promised to cherish and love "until death do us part." The fire-place was empty and unlighted, the chairs and tables strewn round in disorder, litter of paper and tobacco ashes on, the floor, every indication that here an army unit had recently made their quarters.

"Damn this war, this carnage of blood among people of the same race and families!" he exclaimed aloud as he looked around.

There was yet no thought in his mind that the dearest associations of his own life would never again be recalled, except tortured by the memory of the worst features of it imposed upon his own life.

"She'll be in to see you bye and bye," the old man informed him as he withdrew from the room. When next he saw him, he was making his way back to the stable from whence he had first emerged.

Who was the one that would come first? Would it be Flora or her mother, or some other person? He was not long left in doubt. It was the Colonel's wife. Her face was haggard; her eyes shifty; her hair dishevelled.

Lieutenant MacLeod had become inured to many weird and blood-curdling experiences and to face them with stoic calm. But here was one which he neither experienced nor expected. He did not deem it possible that so great a change could come over anyone in so short a time.

"Where is Flora?" he asked tremulously.

"Flora, Flora," she repeated, as one making an effort to recall a forgotten word. In a trice her face brightened as if a new intuition had been granted. Her mind cleared. She came over to him and stood before him with uplifted hand.

"Hector MacLeod, Flora is dead."

"Flora dead!" he repeated, not grasping its significance.

"Yes, she is dead," she repeated, slowly and with emphasis.

"Dead! My Flora dead! Never, never! Do you tell me, is my Flora dead?"

"Hector MacLeod, Flora is dead." Then coming over and taking his hand in both of hers, she continued:

"Hector MacLeod, I have a message of tragic importance to convey to you. I can only deliver it to you on one condition, that you pledge me on your soldier's honour you will never divulge it to any other one of your own race. Will you grant me that pledge?"

Lieutenant MacLeod looked her steadily in the eye.

"If it is anything which I must know and keep secret, then trust me, my pledge is given."

"On your soldier's honour?"

"On my soldier's honour!" he repeated slowly.

"Then I must tell you a brutal crime was attempted by a. Hessian officer, Oscar Rheinhardt, and Flora is dead."

"But was there no one to help and save her?"

The soldier spirit was now the dominant impulse of his will, the vision of a duty which law and order demanded in respect to crime.

"None but Captain MacKenzie."

"And what did he do?"

"He shot for his head, but the bullet only passed through his cheeks and he was saved."

"But didn't he shoot again?"

"The bullet passed through his cheeks and killed Flora."

"My beautiful Flora dead!"

"She is dead, Hector MacLeod," she repeated slowly and with emphasis on each word, "and Rory MacKenzie is a prisoner in the rebel army. He meant well," she said in solemn tone, "but his aim was not straight."

"But, mother,"—it was the first time he had used the word, but she seemed so near and so dear to him now, the mother of his , that all his Scotch reticence was put to immediate flight at the realization of it—"But, mother, Rory was the best shot in the army. How could he have so bungled it?"

Hector MacLeod might have said the best but one, and that one himself, and he would have spoken truth. Why did Captain Mackenzie fail in that gift in which he was most efficient? The answer came from the mother of his young wife, who still held him by the hand.

"Captain MacKenzie could not kill, because his hands were tied. The Avenger of Blood," She whispered fiercely in his ear, as if disclosing an important secret, "is the Next of Kin. Promise me one thing, Hector MacLeod," and she pressed his hand with a vise-like clutch, "Promise me you'll not add crime to crime, but leave it to God."

"No," he answered back revengefully and determinedly, "I cannot and will not promise you that."

"The Avenger of Blood is Next of Kin. He is not here," and she pointed to MacLeod, "But there," and she pointed upwards to Heaven and God. "'Vengeance is mine I'll repay, saith the Lord.' Promise me now! promise me!"

The mother's entreaty became more earnest with every added word she uttered. Hector MacLeod felt an imperative placed upon him by some authority, he knew not why or whence it came.

"You are asking me to do the hardest thing I have ever been asked to do in my life, an impossible thing; no, mother, I cannot promise you that. 'The land cannot' be cleansed of the blood that is shed, but by the blood of him that shed it.' I am the Next of Kin, and it will be for me to demand blood for worse than blood."

"Promise me!" she repeated with increased vehemence and urgency. "Leave to God His own just work! I cannot let you leave my presence until you do."

Again Hector MacLeod felt the imperative placed upon him. It seemed to him that another personality was taking hold of him and making him go the way opposed to his own just judgment.

Following that alien leadership, "Mother, I promise," he answered slowly, almost inaudibly.

"You are noble, but God is just. Trust Him, fear Him, but most of all, obey Him."

Having thus delivered her parting message, she dropped his hands, turned about abruptly, and walked with head erect out of the room.

Hector MacLeod stood alone in that house of loneliness, death and crime. He looked round about him—if only he could see some memento he might take away with him of the light and love which so often warmed his heart. The door to his right was slightly ajar. It was Flora's. He stepped in. The floor was covered with stains of blood—hers and his; hers, the index of loftiest purity and noblest virtue; his, the index of the lowest degradation in crime.

On the bureau by his side he saw a work of embroidery, that upon which her gentle hands had last wrought. He took it up tremblingly, hardly daring to look upon it. It was a half-finished garment of a little babe.

"Hers and mine," he repeated, "if she had lived."

He thurst it gently into his pocket, the memento of a departed love and a lost hope. For a time he stood transfixed to that sacred spot. Passionate anger, revengeful hate and benignant love, each sought a first place in his mind. Which of these three spirits would he exalt to the mastery of his heart and his life? The latter conquered, and the Flora of his youthful life became the taslisman of his manhood and future days.

Just then he heard the blast of a bugle call. The land was a carnage of blood and death. He hastened to his horse. In a trice he was in the saddle and the face of the steed turned armyward. With a leap, the restive beast began a furious gallop in the direction from which it had come.

Suddenly a new mood struck the rider. A word of command and the beast stood still. Hector MacLeod mopped his brow.

"To add to this carnage of blood! For whom?" he asked himself aloud. "For England's German king with his Hessian hirelings, or the rebel colony? I cannot fight now for the one, and I certainly shall not for the other."

Even as he was putting his resolution in audible form, a soldier, dressed in Loyalist garb like himself, was hastening to his side rum his place of hiding in the nearby woods. Beads of sweat stood out numerously and in increasing size on his cold forehead. The fences, fields and woods went swirling before eyes. He felt his strength departing, reeled and fell, but into the arms of Rory MacKenzie, his cousin and helper and friend.

On his return to consciousness he found himself in a secluded woods; a group of soldiers were sitting around him. When memory recalled to him the torturing events of his immediate past, he turned to his cousin and said, "It was the sight of the blood—hers and his—and together—I couldn't stand it." This in explanation of the unsoldiery condition which caused him to fall from his steed.

"But Rory, how was it you didn't make sure work of him? How was it that you missed him and hit Flora?"

"I shoot Flora, Hector? God, forgive me, I haven't been near the place since the day that I left the pistol with her. Who said it was I who killed her?"

"Her mother said so, but she has gone wrong."

The version of the tragedy given by Flora's mother was no doubt prompted by the subtle cunning of an insane mind, the motive to which one can readily understand when they consider the part played by Mrs. MacLean herself in the tragedy.

CHAPTER III

RUSTY BROWN

According to the carefully prepared plans of their parents, Hector MacLeod with his three chums set out on the day appointed for the Penetanguishene, the place of shining sands, where they were to be met by Rusty Brown, an independent trader of the La Cloche and Georgian Bay region, who was to be their guide and protector for the season.

Generous in respect to time, the trader arrived at this half-breed post with a mackinac sailing vessel several hours before the stage, which was to be their medium of travel, was due from Holland Landing. Strolling up into the village, he took a seat on the long bench, placed for the accommodation of its guests on the front of the only public house of the place, a story-and-a-half log building, conducted by a half-breed, Timothy Devine.

"Looks as if the old waggon is not going to get here. to-day, Timothy," was his comment, when after two hours' waiting his host came to the door, and peered down the road to see if there was any sign of its coming.

"Dat stage me not see him come. Too hot day and too beeg load maybe yet. Ha, he come now for sure."

So it was. The heavily laden wagon was being slowly tugged along the road and up the hill by two tired mules, whose angular bones and ribs were thrusting themselves observedly against their skins, in evidence that excessive labour with limited rations was the destiny forced upon them by their driver. Opposite the Devine House the stage came to a full stop.

"Hello there, Rusty! I've brought your bunch with me; four of them," the driver called out, as soon as he had pulled his jaded mules to a. willing halt. "You'll find their baggage there on the back."

Immediately the four youths jumped down from the caravan, one by one, and began looking around to identify the man to whom the driver had spoken.

"Are you Mr. Brown?" Lorne Pentland enquired, as he saw Rusty approaching them.

The trader answered in the affirmative and enquired in turn if they were the boys who were to spend the summer with him on Parry Island.

"That's who we are for sure," Lorne informed him.

Although Hector MacLeod was the nominal head of the group, in the matter of conversation, Lorne was the real leader, or at least the most talkative one.

"I am Lorne Pentland," he continued. It was my father who wrote to you, and these three are the rest of us. The short stout one, that's Alan Cameron; the tall thin fellow, that's Wilfred Opie, and the heavyweight is Hector MacLeod, the head and front of the army."

Lorne pointed his forefinger at each of the boys as he named them. Rusty Brown followed with his eyes and let them rest some time on the countenance of Hector. The boys awaited some further form of salutation from their prospective guide, but there was none. Instead, it was an imperative for their immediate embarkation.

"Better get your luggage, and we'll heave out of here before the wind goes down. There's a splendid breeze now and in the right direction, and we have a considerable journey ahead of us."

"Shall we reach there to-night?" enquired Alan.

"Hardly to-night, but we'll reach a good camping site between here and there before it gets too late."

The first impression left by Rusty Brown on the boys was a favourable one. He must have been a man in the near sixties, though his looks and movements would suggest a much younger man. He wore no hat but his dark auburn locks, with here and there a grey hair, lay in thick curls over his head and provided him ample protection. His eyes were a rich brown. In his general appearance he was tall but slimly built, for though six feet in height he was less than twelve stone in weight. In deportment he was agile, active, alert and walking or standing carried himself as straight and erect as a pine tree. Altogether he gave the impression of one to whom the word handsome would not have been inappropriate in his younger days. His conversation bespoke a. man of culture and training, while in his manner there was something subdued and gentle, a quality of mind attained only by a long training in self-control, all of which indicated a personality for which a less vulgar environment would be more in keeping.

Rusty was his community name, the one attached to him because of the colour of his hair, his eyelashes, his eyebrows and his whiskers. The latter he wore neatly trimmed and combed, a habit contrary to that usually followed by the traders and voyageurs of this north country. Had there been less darkness in their colour, he might have been named "Reddie," but Nature had supplied a sufficient tinge to make "Rusty" the more suitable designation. "Brown" may have been the name of his parents, but more than likely this came to him also, not as a gift from his ancestor but a subsequent acquisition from his fellow-citizens in the woods. At any rate, Rusty Brown was the only name which the annals of the community accorded him.

For the present, whatever his past may have been, his first duty was to get the four youths to Parry Island, and to that undertaking he set himself with ready alacrity.

"Is this your boat?" Lorne enquired, as their guide halted at a spot on the shore opposite a floating sailboat.

"Yes, this is mine," he answered with pride and with a tone which was meant to convey the impression it was a vessel worthy of appreciation.

It was a strongly built mackinac, thirty feet from stem to stem, seven-foot beam, pointed at both bow and stern, and carried two sails with about five hundred feet of canvas. A considerable number of stones lay at the bottom, which their guide informed them was meant for ballast.

In a short time the baggage came, and with other equipment was made up into a neat pile in the centre of the boat. All was now readiness for the trip through the islands to their encampment. Rusty took his seat at the stem, with the helm and one sail under his charge, while Hector was entrusted with the foresail. They started out with full sail and wind astern.

"You call this class of boats mackinacs do you not, Mr. Brown?" was Hector's further remark, whose knowledge of sailing vessels, it would appear, was more extensive than that of any of the other boys, except perhaps Lorne's.

"That's their name, Hector, and this is one of the staunchest of them on the bay. But you'll call me 'Rusty,' not 'Mister,' he enjoined him, placing a peculiar and ironic emphasis on the "Mister." "It's neither 'Brown' nor 'Mister Brown' but plain 'Rusty.' It's the name I've always had here, and it's the one and the only one that suits me best."

"But our habit has been to respect our seniors, Mr. Brown, both in the language we use and our behaviour towards them. In addressing our superiors, we have been taught that it is not becoming to call them by their first name like one of ourselves. 'Mister' is a title of respect."

In his answer, Hector gave expression not only to his own mind but the thought also of the whole camp.

"Custom differs in different places," their guide replied, "and there are no 'Misters' anywhere on these waters. 'Rusty' is my title," he added, emphasizing the pronoun, "so if you'll let me say so, that's what you'll call me."

"If Mr. Brown wants it that way, then let us get used to it," was Lorne's comment and counsel on the matter.

"I don't know," Hector still objected. "Perhaps we'll get so used to it we'll carry the custom back to civilization with 'us. Habit becomes second nature, Mr. Brown."

Hector evinced here a conservatism characteristic of his race, and his reluctance to immediately surrender himself to the manners and customs of their new surroundings did not seem entirely displeasing to their host.

"Rusty" was, as he said, his title. There were many "Browns" but only one "Rusty." The observant public had seized on this one item of his personal appearance and made it the title of his individuality.

In spite of custom, however, the boys wisely, under Hector's leadership, adhered strictly to the code of etiquette under which they had been carefully trained, refusing to surrender themselves to a familiarity, even in language, which could only tend to breed disrespect to one, their superior in age, experience and knowledge. Whether speaking to or of him, the boys maintained a strict adherence to the more befitting title.

As these introductory remarks were passing to and fro, the sailboat was responding gallantly to the favourable breezes blowing from the southwest, their prevailing quarter at this season of the year.

Soon the shoreline from which they disembarked was left far behind, and the boat went driven along northward through the eastern channel, a course which supplied a panorama of beauty, and a variety of islands, second to no other route on the bay.

It was mid-afternoon the next day before they came in sight of the place chosen for their permanent encampment. A large island bred over with thick forest lay ahead of them to their right. Pointing to a high cliff, which seemed to be situated far inland, "That's the place up yonder," their guide informed them.

"Why not have it near the water?" Alan asked, as he saw the distance from which it stood behind the near coast.

"It'll be when you get there," Rusty replied with a twinkle in his eye, as he turned the vessel to the right.

When they drew near the shoreline, the boys observed that instead of an unbroken coast, they were heading towards an opening—a narrow channel not much wider than their boat. Their skipper guided the mackinac with unerring hand, and brought them into what, but for this narrow channel, would have been an inland lake, hidden from view of the outer waters by the high wooded bluffs which surrounded it. Across this basin the breeze wafted them to the far side where was the cliff to which he was guiding them. It stretched far upward towards the sky and appeared to be a part of the deep forest which surrounded it. The boat was beached on a sandy shore underneath a ledge of this rock, overlooking the bay.

In a few minutes the passenger crew had the boat unloaded, and the shore strewed with their baggage and equipment.

"We'll leave these here for a minute," Rusty explained, "while we go up to have a look at the site."

"Strikes me that it is pretty high up," remarked Lorne, as he looked towards the top of the cliff.

"The miskitties are down below and the breezes are above, which would you rather have?" the guide replied with a smile.

He led them by a well-trodden path to the top of the cliff, which they discovered to be an open plateau, covering about half an acre of ground. The rock was of gray granite, and where it was not worn off was covered with deep moss, which yielded to the tread of the foot, as soft as a feather mattress. The stumps round about and the long-fallen trees were also covered with this same sea-green and heathery-purple product of these northern islands. It was an ideal place for their camp, and gave evident signs that it had been frequently used for that purpose.

A chorus of praises greeted the ears of the guide as he exhibited the place of his selection.

The boys began to explore about, noting carefully the preparations which Rusty had made for their accommodation.

Two log-cabins were erected, a large one for their sleeping apartment, and a smaller one for cook and eating house. In both of them crude fireplaces were built of stone, all of which bore testimony to the initiation and resource of their guide.

Hector stood before the door and spelled out the name, "Camp Assiginack," branded in scrawling letters on the wood with a hot iron.

The sun was yet some distance from the horizon, when they had everything in readiness for their first night at Camp Assiginack.

After tea, served by the guide, the boys strolled down to the ledge of rock overlooking; the bay. There they watched the gray and white gulls and the garnets flying about, or resting on the near rocks, while they discussed the programme for their summer camp.

"Early to bed and early to rise," came cheerful counsel of Rusty, as with paddle in hand he started down to the shore at dusk. "I'll paddle over to my hut in your new canoe. To-morrow morning, bright and early, I'll be back to see how you've weathered the night."

The boys ceased their gay conversation and watched Rusty paddle out from the foot of the cliff to his island home opposite to them. They watched him silently until he disappeared in the gloaming.

The silence was broken by the enquiry of Alan. "I wonder if Mr. Brown ever heard a bugle?"

"I doubt it," answered Lorne, "but there could be no harm in sounding out a call or two."

At the suggestion, Alan ran to the cabin and brought a couple. He handed one to Lorne and the other to Wilfred. Wilfred took it indifferently and then passed it over to Hector.

"Give them good and strong, boys." Alan stood expectantly, and somewhat impatiently, awaiting their putting into service the instruments which he so eagerly brought them.

"Single or double?" querried Lorne as he stood up preparatory to granting his request.

"Single first, if you please, Lorne, and slow between the notes that we may get the echo."

"If there happens to be any," Lorne replied as he fitted the mouthpiece on preparatory for action.

The air was motionless. Not a ripple stirred the waters of the Mer Douce. The Echo Elfs were out on every rock and island of the bay. Call after call was sounded forth by Lorne and Hector alternately.

Rusty was drawing near the shore of his island home when the first blast of Lorne's bugle reached his ear. Then, soft and mellow, the same sound echoed from the far rock before him, so that to Rusty in the canoe it seemed seemed as if two bugles were sounding. He ceased his paddling and listened reverently—the Last Post—Lights Out—how strange and eerie! When the last note died away, he paddled the remaining distance quietly, lest he should desecrate the solitude, never to him so uncanny before.

When the bugle sound of the "Last Post" passed over the waters and echoed back from the far rock, it was something more to Rusty Brown than the sound of a bugle. It was symbolic of the passing out of an old era and the ushering in of a new. Rusty Brown represented one generation—those pioneers who laid themselves upon the altar of sacrifice in an environment beneath their station in order that they might lay the foundations of a new and higher era of progress and civilization for the generations following them. The four youthful collegians represented another generation. They were the forerunners of that annual stream of tourists who were to wrest these islands from the silent solitude in which they had lain undisturbed for ages and make of them the habitations of noisy city dwellers, resorts for recreation, health and pleasure every summer month, enjoying the varieties of their scenic beauty as they inhaled the pure invigorating air and the health-giving ozone of these northern latitudes.

The boys walked quietly back to the cabin after having exhausted their list of calls, with a view to making preparation for their night's rest.

Although it was July, and although contrary to the reckoning of all their former experiences, at this season of the year there was a marked chilliness in the night air which suggested to Wilfred a fire in the grate.

"What say you, Hector, to a fire? This is an ideal night for one. Shall we start one going?"

"It's either a. fire, or sweaters, or our cots for the night. What say you all?" asked their leader.

A fire was voted unanimously.

Soon the fuel was gathered and a goodly fire started, which lighted up the whole room with its cheerful blaze. Sitting before it they discussed many things, but chiefly their protector and guide.

"'Rusty'! Do you think is that his right name?"

It was Wilfred Opie who expressed this enquiry.

"It certainly is not," asserted Lorne with dogmatic certainty.

"What a wasted life his must have been, for he says he has spent the most of it in the woods," continued Wilfred. "The wind, the woods, the sea and the night, his only companions apart from the Indians."

"Perhaps he may have had compensations," Hector observed.

"Compensations! What compensation could there be for what he has lost by burying himself out here away from his equals, and every opportunity and comfort of civilized life?" Wilfred could see only sacrifice and nothing of gain in the life of the frontiersman.

"Perhaps he is a poet or artist," interjected Alan, "dreaming his dreams and enjoying the dream but having no aspiration to Change the dream into a reality of life."

"Far from that," Hector replied. "He is not the dreaming kind; too much restless movement for that. He would make a better soldier than an artist."

"Soldier! Now you have struck the peg, Hector," exclaimed Lorne in happy agreement with him. "Soldier! That's what he is, an 1812 or Revolutionary soldier. Watch his step when next he approaches and see if I'm not right."

"And the curl of his air and see if I'm not right," added Alan, expressing his judgment on the matter.

"And the dolor of his eyes and see if I'm not right," was Wilfred's comment.

As a matter of fact all three were right, for in that one personality known from Fort William to Penetang as Rusty Brown, there was embodied the trinity of natural endowments which qualified him to be soldier, artist or poet, and in all three avocations he had at one time or another played a not unimportant part.

When the discussion was ended, with the light of the fireplace, Wilfred read the Bible lesson and prayer for the night, after which each one betook himself to his respective cot.

In a short time a deep quiet reigned in the cabin as exhausted nature sought to restore itself in gentle sleep. All around outside a similar stillness reigned, save for the recurrent notes of a nearby whip-poor-will, whose audible meditations were answered by a mate on a distant tree, in the same notes and tone;

A beagle pup, a gift of Rusty's to the camp, walked up and down, surveying each cot and then crawling up on that of Hector's, was the last of the sacred group to pass away into unconscious and dreamless sleep.

CHAPTER IV

A BIRD OF ILL OMEN

The summer passed rapidly by for the four boys on Parry Island. The days came and went in hurried succession. Canoeing, fishing and hunting— these, alternating with the more serious pastime of studying the flora of the district and mounting exhibits of fish and birds—comprised the rounds of their regular recreations. Rusty Brown had proved the most companionable of guides and equally informing in respect to the flora and geology of the neighbourhood. A few days more, then they would be ready to strike tents and return home to their studies for the Winter.

"What about a fishing trip to-day?" Wilfred Opie suggested on the Monday morning of their last week on the island. "I should judge this to be a good day; so still and calm."

"Fishing let it be," assented Lorne.

"Salmon or pickerel—what would you suggest, Mr. Brown?"

The boys always consulted their guide and followed his counsels on every occasion.

"It ought to be a good day for salmon trawling," he answered. "I think we might go to the east inlet and spend the afternoon there."

"What about duck? Any duck in that region?" enquired Alan.

"Duck may be found anywhere now" The ones hatched here are beginning to flock, preparatory to going south, but the north ones haven't come in yet. They'll not reach here until the cold weather sets in. There were several flocks of Mallards hatched at the east inlet this summer. We might get a pair for your collection if we remained there long enough."

"What shall we take—your sailboat or our canoe?" Lorne enquired.

"The canoe, I think, would be best," replied the Guide.

"Oh, but say," interjected Alan, "this is the day that Little Knife comes with the venison and he has promised us a day's hunting before we go back. That means we shall have to postpone our trip for to-day."

"Not necessarily, Alan. "It was Hector who spoke. "I'll stay and look after the venison and entertain Little Knife with promises of mallard and salmon when you get back."

"No, you don't," all three boys answered in chorus.

"It's all for the trip or none," urged Wilfred.

"Division of labour is the law of the camp," answered Hector. "What's your excursion to-day will be mine to-morrow. It would, besides, be more to my liking that I should stay at home and hear how Little file and his band wrested Michilimackinac from the Americans than it would be for me to go to the Point and spend the afternoon there sealing salmon for our to-morrow's breakfast."

"In which case," observed Alan, "that would be doing nothing, seeing that salmon haven't any scales."

"Perhaps you could persuade the Chief to sit for a drawing," suggested Wilfred. "A portrait of so quaint a figure would be a very interesting souvenir to take back with us to civilization."

"By all means, and with his hair standing as becometh a true-bred Ottawa," added Alan.

"And wearing the sword which the Canadian Commandant gave him for his kindness to our wounded American countryman," Lorne supplied as a further counsel for his guidance.

After considerable discussion to solve the problem arising from the promised visit of Little Knife, it was finally concluded that Hector should remain behind as he had suggested while the rest of them would spend the afternoon at the east end of the inlet in quest of duck and fish.

Although the morning opened out auspiciously, before mid-day the sky began to show evidences of a change in the weather.

"I'm afraid," their guide observed as they were starting out, "that it is not going to be too promising an afternoon for our trip after all. Those clouds to the south are quite black and heavy. I've seen storms come up with less warning."

His misgivings proved to be well founded. It was in—the middle of the afternoon when Alan, who had been still-fishing on the point where they had landed, heard a shout from his companions.

"Bring over the canoe! Hurry! There's a storm coming."

Looking up and scanning the sky to the south, he observed the heavy black clouds which had been hovering there all the afternoon now moving rapidly northward, carried forward by a strong heavy wind, which was increasing in velocity the nearer it travelled towards them.

In quick obedience he launched the canoe and paddled hurriedly over to where they were. As soon as he reached them, all three jumped into the canoe and began to paddle together strongly in the direction of their camp.

"We'll never make it," remarked Alan, as he contrasted the rapidity with which the storm was coming and the long distance they had yet to paddle to reach the camp.

"Hardly likely," added Lorne.

The black clouds were now over their head. Behind them the bay, which all morning had lain like a sea of glass, was now suddenly transformed into a succession of white-capped waves, all of which were rolling forward in an apparent attempt to overtake the canoe. In the clouds above, unseen, yet heard in the form of thunderous roars, waves of electricity dashed themselves to pieces against the walls of water which impeded their further progress. Lightning streaks danced merrily here and there and everywhere on the surface of the clouds now reaching down closer to the earth.

"Let us make for the nearest shore," Rusty Brown counselled with no little concern, as he saw how rapidly the storm was approaching them. "We can take shelter under that rock if we can make a safe landing."

As soon as the suggestion was made the canoe was turned shoreward. Before them was a rock shore slanting slowly and smoothly to the water line. In calm weather it was well enough suited for a landing place, but in a storm and washed with the incoming waves, great care would have to be exercised to effect a safe landing. The canoe and the storm reached the shore together. The first wave caught their light barque, flung it forward on the rock, and although all four were drenched as the wave broke and splashed over them, yet, luckily, opportunity was given them to save themselves. Before the second wave arrived, Alan, with an alacrity suited to the occasion, lifted himself out of the canoe and firmly planted on a good footing held on while the others followed in quick succession, his example.

As soon as they were landed, the quartette, two on each side, took hold of the canoe and carried it forward until they deemed it was a safe distance set inward from the shore line.

The storm came on apace. They crept under a large ledge of an overhanging rock and from their place of refuge watched the bay lashed into its fiercest fury. The tall trees round about were bending and creaking, while here and there one, which could not stand the strain of the tempest, went down with a crash. A nearby pine, that had defied the changing moods of seasons and weather for more than a century, was struck by lightning, and the flying splinters fell all around them. They had made good selection of their place of refuge, and so remained unhurt, but the canoe suffered a. different fate. The coming of the storm blew the waters of the bay far up on the shore and lifted it from its mooring place to become the helpless victim of every succeeding wave.

"There's our canoe gone," exclaimed Lorne, as he saw it carried out from the shore.

"We'll get it again," answered Alan. "It'll not go out very far as long as the wind stays where it is now."

"That wind seems to be coming from all sides. Those three trees over there have each fallen in a different direction."

"And the rain—see it come!" For a full half-hour it poured down in torrents, then spent itself as quickly as it arose. The clouds were soon dispersed, the sky cleared, the westering sun shone down in its usual brightness, and every water-drop on the became a sparkling diamond holding in little globular body the seven colours of the rainbow.

As soon as the storm passed over, the question of how they were to get back to the camp became the uppermost thought in their mind.

Coming out of their place of safety and looking for the whereabouts of the canoe, they observed it dancing on the surface a little distance out from the shore, drifting parallel with it but in the opposite way from the camp.

"Shall I swim out and bring it in?" Alan asked, when he saw how near it was to land.

"Not in a sea like that," answered Rusty Brown.

The Wind which came from the south in the beginning of the storm had now veered and was blowing from the west.

"It is quite choppy, but I think I can make it. It's a pity to see it lost, when I am sure I could bring it in."

"Perhaps, but it is not worth the risk. The canoe can be replaced but your life could not be."

"What shall we do then?"

"After the waters are settled, we'll come back with the sailboat and pick it up, but in the meantime we'll trek it home on land. It may be rough walking, but it will be safe."

They started along the difficult shore line to make their way back to the camp. It was late before they arrived.

"I wonder where is Hector?" they asked one another, when they arrived and did not observe him anywhere around, but instead the door of the cabin open, the floor wet from the rain, and some articles of their furniture overturned with the wind.

"Run to the shore and see if my canoe is there," Rusty instructed Alan.

"The canoe is here," Alan shouted from the shore, after he had gone to the beach and saw it safely hidden away in its accustomed place among the bushes.

"Then he is somewhere around unless he has gone off with Little Knife," was the further comment of their guide. "That was a bad storm, boys—a veer, and this island seems to have been the centre of it. Take your gun Wilfred and fire a shot. The boy can't be far away."

"Our gun is in the canoe, but we'll use yours," Wilfred replied as he hastened to the cabin to obtain that fieldpiece.

"The gun is gone," he shouted from doorway, after he had made a search and discovered its absence.

On hearing this, the countenance of Rusty Brown lowered appreciably. "That was a bad storm," he again repeated. "There were a lot of trees went down, yes, hundreds of them."

Wilfred sensed the drift of their protector's thoughts.

"Do you think, would there be such a thing as Hector getting struck with a limb of a tree?" There was a. tremor of anxiety in his voice as he asked this question of Rusty.

The evidences of the truth of Rusty's remarks and the destructive work of the storm were seen all around them. The absence of Hector under such circumstances could not be anything other than the cause of grave concern to the camp.

"We must get out and look for him," intimated Wilfred, whose nervous fear increased with every minute which passed without Hector putting in an appearance.

"We must explore all around the camp at once and see if we can get any trace of him."

"I think I'll try the bugle first," said Lorne, suiting the action to the word.

Going out on the peak of the rock he sounded out call after call, pausing between times, peradventure a response would come from their lost companion. But there was none. The swish of the waves on the rock was the only answer.

When the bugle calls brought no response, Lorne joined Rusty, Wilfred and Alan, who in the meantime, were exploring the shore line and the woods in the immediate neighbourhood of the camp, lest a falling tree or a limb should be held accountable for his absence. This they continued until the darkness of the night made further search impossible.

"I think we had better build a signal fire" suggested Rusty, after all four were returned from their unsuccessful attempt to locate his whereabouts. "It would be a good place to build it on the peak of the rock, then he could see it if he happened to be anywhere along the shore of the bay."

The suggestion was no sooner made than , the boys began to carry it out. In a short time the wood was gathered, and soon the flames of a huge bonfire mounted high up in the air, which could not be other than plainly seen far over the waters.

The fire being built they now began to discuss the cause of his absence.

"He's off with Little Knife somewhere," was the judgment expressed by Rusty Brown. "The gun is gone, and Little Knife's canoe is not here, and so he must be away with him."

After giving expression to this opinion, Rusty arose, and going into the cabin began to prepare for the boys a belated supper.

When they sat down, "Where is the beagle?" enquired Wilfred.

"Wasn't she here when we came back?" asked their guide.

"Yes," answered Wilfred, "but she must have gone off somewhere since."

"Call her," he instructed Lorne.

Lorne went to the door and whistled repeatedly but there was no response from the mascot.

"Looks as if she's gone off to hunt for Hector," commented Alan. "You know she always preferred him to the rest of us."

"But that breaks down my theory that he is off with Little Knife," was Rusty Brown's thought on the matter, "unless both of them are stranded somewhere on the shore near here."

The absence of the beagle but increased the perplexity of the camp. After supper all four came back to the signal fire and sat around it in silence, but with ears alert in hopes that by some good chance Hector might turn up from somewhere.

After a time a footstep was heard on the shore.

"Hector!" the three boys exclaimed and went to meet him.

It was not he, but Chief Little Knife, who was guided to the place by their signal fire.

"Where is Hector?" they asked him.

"Me not know; me not see him," the Indian answered.

"Was he not with you? Weren't you here before to—day?"

"No, me not here before to-day."

"You not here? Then Hector must have gone off alone."

This did not improve but rather increased the gravity of the occasion.

"One of our boys is lost," Rusty informed the chief in order to explain the reason for their many questions.

"Boy lost! That's bad. On the bay?" in enquired eagerly.

"We do not know," Lorne answered. "We were out for the afternoon, but when we came back he was not here."

"That a bad wind, the worst ever me see. Lots of tree go down." The Indian looked about him and observed the devastating work which had been done in the near neighbourhood of the camp.

"Were you out in it?" enquired Rusty.

"Ugh," he grunted, and shrugged his shoulders. "Feel him."

Rusty put out his hand and felt his clothes. They were still wet.

"I make for shore and land me good, but rain come down, and tree smash and fall all around me. But that's bad the boy away."

"Do you suppose he could have been struck with a tree?" Wilfred again asked with increased concern, the fear of which now more deeply impressed him as he listened to the Indian's version of his own experiences.

No one ventured an answer to Wilfred's question. The Indian took a position as close as possible to the fire, followed by the others, who sat around it, silently watching the fantastic figures which the flames described.

Through the night, as a green log, which the Indian had thrown on the fire, was spitting and sputtering, they saw arising, as it were, the figure of a sailing vessel, a mackinac, not unlike the one that Rusty owned.

"A boat," the Indian observed, as the figure stood out so clearly delineated before them.

"Did you ever see anything like it!" exclaimed Alan, as he looked upon the picture made by the emitting clouds of steam and smoke arising from the burning log.

"Sails and all—a perfect picture!" Lorne added.

"That your boat, Rusty?" observed the Indian, as the likeness continued unabated in clearness before them.

But the trader sat silent, gazing solemnly at the apparition, yet offering no word of comment as to its likeness to his own.

After a long period of silence, and as if ignoring the appearance of the phantom ship he brought up again the subject of the afternoon's storm.

"That certainly was a storm; the worst I ever saw on these waters."

After some pause, a second observation, "I experienced only one like it," was added.

After this remark there was a still longer period of silence when all at once as if forgetful of the phantom ship in the fire, he turned to the Indian, and asked with unexpected abruptness, "Do you know what day is this, Knife?"

The Indian kept looking into the fire, but ventured no answer, deeming no doubt that none was required.

"This is the fifth, Little Knife. And do you know what happened on this day? This is the fifth of October, Little Knife."

The deep black of the Indian's eyes were lighted up with an animated expression as he looked up and met the gaze of Rusty Brown.

"Dis the fiff? Yes, dis de day Tecumseh, he die."

"Yes, this is the day, the anniversary of the death of Tecumseh, Little Knife. And do you remember how Captain Mackenzie, standing among you Indians and seeing the Chief fall, said, 'Little Knife, the Americans have offered a. reward for the body of Tecumseh, dead or alive'?"

"Yeh, me know."

"Don't you remember Captain Mackenzie saying to you and Conossoway, 'Little Knife, the Americans will never get him. No, sir, they will not'?"

"Yeh, yeh, me know."

"And you remember how he yelled at you Indians, 'Come On!' and how you surrounded Tecumseh and drove Johnson back?"

"Yeh, yeh, me there; me come."

"And the Americans didn't get Tecumseh, did they?"

"Dey didn't get Tecumseh," Little Knife repeated after him.

"And they never will, Little Knife."

"No, no, never will," repeated the Indian.

"And do you remember anything else that happened on this day, a. year before that?"

Again he paused for an answer, but there was none coming.

"This is the day, Little Knife, that you brought Rheinhardt wounded to the Commandant. You've got the sword which the Commandant gave you for that kindness. You've got the letter."

"Yeh, me have."

"And you got it because you were kind. That was right, Little Knife. You saved a man that ought to have been killed and couldn't be killed because he was wounded and helpless. That was war as a true Canadian fights it. That was kindness as a Canadian shows it. And you have got the letter?"

"Yeh, yeh, the letter, me have the letter."

The reference was to the recognition given Chief Little Knife of a silver-mounted sword by the Canadian Commandant at Fort Michilimackinac in appreciation of having saved from the scalping knife a wounded American officer and brought him with safety into the fort as a prisoner of war. The letter, expressing this appreciation, was presented to the Chief and both of these have been carefully kept as heirlooms by his family.

"And do you remember anything else which happened on this day?"

The Indian looked at him with a. pleased and animated expression. The boys were now all attention, forgetting for the time being the absence of Hector and the phantom ship in the fire.

"That was the day on which Hector MacLeod's mackinac went down," the modulation of Rusty Brown's voice was now coming down to its usual normal tone.

". . . that mackinac we saw in the fire."

He turned to the boys as he made this added comment on the significance of figure which they had seen.

"And," he paused as he turned again his face towards the Indian, "he got the flour and the pork to the Fort, didn't he, Little Knife?"

"Yeh, yeh, and dey be long time hungry den."

"Yes, we got there in the nick of time, but we got there—and that boat has come back

to-night to tell us to have faith, yes faith in God. We'll get the boy; yes, yes, we'll get the boy," he repeated, and rose up, and threw another log on the fire.

Hardly had these words fallen from the lips of Rusty Brown, when from a nearby hemlock tree there sounded forth the melancholy hoot of an owl. We do not know why frontiersmen have at all times classed this bird as one of ill-omen, yet such has been their almost universal superstition. It was so in this instance. Coming out of the darkness and breaking in so unexpectedly upon the silent stillness following his assuring remarks the sound seemed ominous. The Indian looked at him and he in turn at the Indian, but neither exchanged a word, yet both knew what the other thought. It had a markedly depreciating effect on the faith of the Guide. Again he repeated, "We shall find the boy."

His words were the words of faith but the tone of his voice betrayed a spirit wrestling with doubt, and doubt fast attaining unto the ascendency.

In a subdued tone of voice begotten by the incident, "Boys, you had better make for your cabin and sleep your sleep," he instructed. "Little Knife and I will look after the fire and lay our plans for to-morrow."

CHAPTER V

A PERIOD OF MIST AND MYSTERY

Following the counsel given them, the three boys rose up and slowly wended their way to the cabin, walking side by side, the silence of their surroundings disturbed only by the moaning hoot of the owl, Whose dismal voice continued to break at intervals the stillness of the whole night.

In a few moment afterwards, Lorne turned with a shovel in his hand. "I think we'll light the fireplace. The air is chilly and the cabin damp."

Suiting the action to the word, he gathered up some live coals, and soon had a comfortable fire started. Around this, and sheltered from the damp and cold of the outside air, the boys, their minds too alert for sleep, sat throughout the whole night, awaiting the coming of daylight in order that they might continue their search for their lost companion.

Morning came, but the prospect of discovering the whereabouts of Hector were no better than they were through the night. A heavy and thick mist lay on the surface of the island, and on the waters round about. So deep was this that it was all one whether it were night or day. There was nothing to do but to await until the fog lifted. As they sat around, impatient and restless, there was one of them who was more impatient than all the rest. It was Wilfred.

Hector and Wilfred had grown up together as playmates, knowing no other companions until the day they both started out to college. In outward appearance they were now the very opposite of one another. Hector was a heavily built youth, tall, muscular, capable of great physical tasks, and lacking nothing in the power of continued endurance, Wilfred, on the other hand, though tall, taller even than Hector, was in weight far below that which his height warranted, but he possessed a pertinacity of endurance that belied his appearance.

Both of these boys excelled in outdoor sports, and both showed a keen aptitude for study. Best of all both were ambitious to make a success of life by investing to the best possible advantage their inherited gifts; yet, While the aim of each was equally commendable, the predilections of Wilfred pointed out for him a different career from that of Hector.

"Give to the people comfortable and happy homes, and healthy bodies with which to enjoy them," said Hector.

"Give to the people right ideas of life and right principles to regulate their conduct," answered Wilfred.

So each of them, according to his viewpoint, had now started out to shape his future destiny and had entered a training college, Hector choosing medicine for his profession, but Wilfred the Christian ministry.

In the experiences of life, misfortune seemed to have dogged the path of Wilfred. At six years of age his mother died, and his memory of her was to him ever after a pleasant dream. Her artistic tastes and traits of disposition found a perfect reproduction in her son. After the loss of his mother, the domestic life of Wilfred was one continued succession of housekeepers and governesses, all strongly opinionated as to the best methods of rearing an only child, but all equally destitute of the milk of human kindness, the first essential to its successful accomplishment. The one bright spot in his life throughout these years, was the companionship and friendship of his cousin, Hector.

That Wilfred was feeling keenly the unexplained absence of Hector was evidently manifest. In the middle of the morning, he arose and announced that he was going out into the woods, fog or no fog.

"You his brudder?" the Indian asked.

"No, but his cousin and chum," answered Wilfred,

"Me see," and the Indian nodded his head, as in this he found the explanation of his deeper anxiety concerning Hector's absence.

When Rusty Brown saw the growing restlessness of Wilfred, and himself also anxious to do something towards solving the cause of Hector's disappearance, he turned to the Indian and said, "I think we had better take a canoe and go to your village to get chief send some of his men over to help us search the woods just as soon as the fog lifts."

Lorne seconded the proposal heartily.

"That is right, Mr. Brown. We can't be searching the woods just now but that is something we can do."

Rusty went to the door, for they were all inside the cabin, save when one went out to put more wood on the signal fire.

"It is pitch black," he said, as he looked out towards the waters, but I think someone ought to take a chance on it."

The Indian rose up, and tieing his sash a little tighter around his waist, pointed to Wilfred and said, "Me take him in my canoe."

"No, no," answered Rusty with emphasis. "One boy is gone now, and trouble never comes by itself alone on this bay. We have had one spell of ill-luck, and there's no telling of what may happen next. I'll go myself but not the boys."

"Oh, pshaw! We're not cowards," protested Wilfred. "I'm quite willing to go with the chief and I think he'll take me there and back safely."

"Sure, me bring you back," the Indian asserted.

"I'm with you, Wilfred," interjected Lorne. "A fog may be bad for schooners in shallow waters and among rock islands but nothing can happen to a canoe on a still day no matter how foggy."

"And I, too," added Alan.

The matter of fact was that the boys were heartily tired of sitting around doing nothing and they welcomed any suggestion which would give them something to do towards finding their lost comrade.

"I don't think it is right for you boys go," asserted their guide. "Either let Little Knife go alone, or I'll go with him, and you boys stay and keep up the fire."

"Me all right with boy. Me go and come back to-night." The Indian had set his mind on having Wilfred with him.

Finally Rusty Brown assented to his going with Little Knife to acquaint them of their misfortune that they might begin a thorough search of the woods as soon as the fog lifted.

The three went down to the shore to see them off. Rusty slipped several pieces of tobacco into Little Knife's hand.

"Pass it round, Little Knife, when you get over to the village," he enjoined.

"They'll never get back here before night," remarked Lorne, as he saw them disappear into the mist before they had made two lengths' distance of their canoe. "Why the fog is now so thick you could cut it with a knife."

"It's going to be dark without doubt." was something of misgiving in Rusty's mind as he made this remark, but as if to reassure himself he added, "These Indians have great instinct. When you get a careful one, it's seldom anything happens. I think they'll make the trip all right."

"They can't get drowned anyway," was the comment of Alan, observing how calm the water was.

The three stumbled back to the camp under the helpful guidance of their signal fire.

"We shall need to get more wood gathered so as to have it ready for to-night," Rusty remarked as he threw a fresh log on the blaze. "The beagle hasn't come back, has she?"

This he asked not expecting an answer, but as an expression of the passing thought of his own mind.

"She must have found him, wherever he is," added Alan.

"He can't be far away, when she knew where to find him, though the instinct of these dumb animals is sometimes marvellous," continued their guide. "He's somewhere on the island, that is certain or she would have been back before this."

"Strange, isn't it, Mr. Brown, that in life troubles never come singly, as you observed a while ago," remarked Alan, as they sat before the fireplace waiting for the return of the Indian and Wilfred. "First there was the storm and the loss of our canoe; then Hector away, and now the fog, so that we can't even go out to look for him. It is surely strange that the fog hasn't lifted before this."

"It was last night's cold that did it," Rusty offered as an explanation. He observed the one follow the other so frequently that he concluded, the one was the cause, the other the effect. "The cold always brings down the clouds. I have seen it stay this way for three days."

This cheerless statement of Rusty's concerning the habits of the weather did little to lessen the burden of anxiety resting on the minds of the boys whose spirits were beginning to rebel against the continued circumstances which compelled them to sit around the camp helpless.

"If only the Chief would come back with the Indians, we might start something going even if it were only more fires here and there on the shore."

"What's that I see there on the water? Isn't that a light?" exclaimed Lorne, as he went to the door and peered out for the twentieth time during the last hour.

A dim flicker in the gray mist was seen roaming along skirting the shore. It was followed by another. "Two, three, four, five, six," the boys counted.

"It's the Indians," explained Rusty. "They're using pine knots."

"I suppose that's for torches," broke in Lorne.

"Yes, they use them for fishing and sometimes for going through the fog. They can manage with these if they are following near the coast."

"Why couldn't we do the same on land and use them to show us through the bush," suggested Lorne.

"They might be all right along the shore, if Hector happened to be marooned anywhere there, but they couldn't do much for us in the woods," answered Rusty.

Soon the Indians' voices were heard as they landed on the beach; two dozen of them, headed by the chief.

They came and sat in a circle around the fire, awaiting, as their manner is, some oracle to guide them in their future course.

The arrival of such a host seemed to lighten the burden of anxiety resting on the minds of the boys. Somehow, they were inspirited in seeing so many stalwart sons of the wilderness coming to help them take

40

up the task of discovering their lost chum. Rusty observed with pleasure the improvement in their spirit.

"It's a good thing that I thought about it," he said to himself as he went about distributing tobacco amongst them, an ample supply of which, thanks to his frugal habits, he possessed.

The impulse to call the Indians to their aid, Rusty considered, was brought to his mind by powers not his own.

"Yesterday it was 'Ill-luck'; to-morrow it will be 'Good-luck,'" he said to the boys, by way of further encouragement.

It was agreed that the Indians should begin at once to patrol the shore in their canoes with the aid of their torches. Two of them went even so far east that they reached the limits of the island on that side, but without results.

Camp fires were then started here and there along the shore where the Indians built themselves huts of evergreen boughs and spent the night awaiting the return of morning and the dissipating of the fog and its darkness.

But the second morning came out still dark and misty. Tears of disappointment welled into Wilfred's eyes as he saw the fog yet hanging heavily over the island. Little Knife, the Indian, was moved with sympathy.

"Wait a bit," he said. "the wind she rise in a little and we see."

"But the wind may not rise to-day, and he may be lying near the camp, perhaps suffering pain," answered Wilfred.

"The wind she rise," the Indian repeated.

"How can you know?" the youth enquired.

"Poplar tree tell me."

It was even so. The leaves of a nearby poplar were beginning to move. The thinness of the stems of the leaves of these trees makes them very sensitive to the least motion in the atmosphere, so that their rustle will be heard often when there is not the slightest indication anywhere else of a rising wind. In a short while, as the Indian prophesied, a rising breeze dissipated the mist, and they were able to begin patrolling the near woods in their search for Hector.

Before starting out, they discussed together their best method of procedure.

"What would be the matter with our describing several straight lines from the camp into the bush, like the spokes of a wheel, and in this way, we would be able to go over the ground on the cliff and around it so as not to overlook any place?"

This was the suggestion of Wilfred who had been ruminating in his mind all morning what best method to follow to secure the most thorough results.

"We could do that quite easily," replied Rusty.

Then, turning to the Indian Chief, he instructed him as to their intended method of procedure.

The chief took his men and divided them to pairs, and began at once to explore the woods in the manner suggested by Wilfred. In this way, by nightfall, they had thoroughly searched a semi-circular area around the tent of more than a mile radius, and had also patrolled the shore, throughout the whole circumference of the island, yet no signs of his whereabouts.

The sun rose up the third morning in a clear sky. "Now," said Lorne, "if Hector is anywhere around and well, he will be able to locate himself and get back to the camp."

"I am not sure of that," answered Rusty Brown. "He has been away a long time without food, and the weather has been very disagreeable; but, if he doesn't come out himself, we ought to be able to find him. If not alive," he added slowly, "we ought to know, at any rate, what has happened to him."

They had planned that this day should be spent in the search of the swamp. It was here that Rusty felt certain that he would be found, as he clung to the thought that he had gone there in quest of cranberries, where a plentiful supply of them were to be found growing in a beaver-meadow located in the centre of it. Hector had gone there on several occasions alone, since it was not far distant from the camp, and Rusty concluded that he had gone there on this occasion also. All the forenoon they circled round and through the jungles of its underwood, until they had patrolled every square yard of it, but still no Hector.

In the afternoon Rusty Brown started out with some of the Indians to the eastern end of the island to explore that district as they had done the vicinity of their cabin and the swamp. The three boys with Little Knife and the rest of the Indians took the opposite direction. It was not long until they came to a trail crossing the island. Turning to the right they followed this until they discovered an Indian hut. This the Indian explored and came out with Rusty's gun in his hand. Here was evidence that Hector, or someone else, had been in this wigwam, and had left the gun there. On more careful examination, they discovered signs of a recent fire, and other evidences of occupation.

There was now great excitement among boys. They started out again following the same trail until they reached the shore on the far side of the island from their camp. Allan was in the lead.

"What's this?" he called out excitedly. "The Beagle, boys! Poor thing, she is dead."

They all rushed to the spot. There lay the little creature stretched out on the sand, with blood oozing from her nose. She was dead, but only recently, for her body was not yet stiff. And what was more, footsteps, which bore evident testimony that Hector also recently had been there.

"Hector's for sure," Wilfred exclaimed as he examined them.

"They are like his," rejoined Lorne.

"But they are his," repeated Wilfred with certitude. "His shoes and mine are mates. We bought them together and there was no difference."

He placed his foot down by the side of one of those shoeprints and reproduced an exact counterpart.

A little further on they came to some additional marks, but these even more puzzling than those already discovered—a place where Hector had apparently been lying stretched on the sand. Around this spot were footmarks of two other persons seen, one wearing moccasins of large dimensions and the other apparently American river boots.

"This moccasin track must be that of a big Indian; I wonder if any of our men have been here to-day, and have found him," Alan remarked as he kept investigating and examining each one separately.

They followed the footmarks to the water line.

"They have gone off in a canoe," Lorne judged as he saw the marks of two canoes having been beached on the shore—or one canoe twice landed—with the footmarks of the two going backward and forward, now in the one, then to the other.

After the boys had made careful examination, it was arranged that watch should be kept on the spot by Lorne and Wilfred and Little Knife, while Alan would go back with the news to Rusty Brown.

It was late in the afternoon when Mr., Brown was returned to the camp where Alan was waiting for him with the news of the discovery of the Beagle and the significant marks on the sand and on the shoreline of the beach.

Greatly excited, "We'll away at once and examine the place," he said, and started hurriedly for the place. On arrival he examined minutely every mark and soon convinced himself that the boys were right and that Hector had been there.

"Poor fellow! He's been lying down here," he said as he saw the tell-tale evidence of it on the sand,

"Is it long since, do you suppose, Mr. Brown?" Wilfred enquired.

"Can't be very long. The marks are too fresh for that. He may have fallen exhausted after coming out of the bush, but what could have killed the poor Beagle? Hector has apparently come down the trail and fallen here for some reason, perhaps exhaustion."

At this juncture the village Chief, with a small band of his men, appeared from the northwestern shore of the island, which they had carefully and minutely explored. They reported a camp of two Wyandot Indians on the shoreline about a mile distant, who had volunteered them the information that the boy had been drowned. Rusty, with the Chief, and Lorne and Alan repaired immediately to the place. When they saw the men, and had observed their foot-gear, they were convinced that these were the two, who marks along with Hector's, were seen on the beach.

"Him dead," the young man answered immediately, "drowned in a canoe."

"How do you know?"

"Saw the canoe go out and out on the bay and then went down."

Further information than this they could not get. The Indian acknowledged seeing the lad, but was absolutely tongue-tied when he was asked to explain the significance of the marks which they had seen on the shore.

CHAPTER VI

A DAY OF FATE FOR HECTOR MACLEOD

"Behold how great a matter a little fire kindleth."

Where was Hector and why absent? This was the question which his companions asked, but to which they could get no answer.

But to Hector himself there was no mystery as to the cause of his disappearance. A short time preceding the storm, a spruce partridge, a species smaller than the birch partridge but exceedingly beautiful, alighted near the lodge and began to pick some of the discarded food from the camp table. Though this was the first of its kind that Hector had seen, yet he had no difficulty in determining its genus from the descriptions given by Rusty at different times when enumerating the classes of birds to be found in the district.

He stood quietly still, watching its appearance and movements with increasing delight, "If I could capture it," he thought, "what a splendid addition it would make to our mounted collection. It will be the finest trophy of the season and I must get it."

The bird stood out in the open with nothing to obscure its view, and Hector assured himself that if it only remained there until he brought out a gun he could easily secure it. There was only Rusty's left, a muzzle-loading, single barreled fieldpiece, fired with percussion cap.

He moved quietly as he went to get it, but the partridge, as if by instinct sensing what was in his mind, became alarmed concerning its safety, and when he got back was running to a place of hiding in a near-by thicket, Cautiously, Hector followed after it, but the now wary bird, according to its habit, began to run hurriedly under cover of the bushes, playing with him from thicket to thicket, a continued game of hide-and-seek, It was only when passing from one clump of undergrowth to the next that it came at all under his observation and then only for a second, until at last, after a long and persistent Chase, it hopped up on a fallen tree which lay across its chosen path.

"Now or never," Hector concluded as he saw it stretch its neck preparatory to flying out of danger's reach into the thick wood. Levelling his gun quickly, he took aim and fired. The percussion cap exploded, but not to his great disgust, the powder, which apparently had not been made to reach the top of the nipple when being loaded.

"How foolish and careless I was not to have examined to see that everything was right," he soliloquized, as he listened with keen disappointment to the whirr of the partridge's wings flying away into the far-off woods.

But something of moment was at that time transpiring which was destined to have more ominous consequence on his immediate failure than the failure to obtain the object of his quest. Away to the south, the sky was rapidly darkening, the presage of a storm which was even at the very time endangering the lives of his companions on the water.

"What's that?" he thought audibly, as he saw the darkness, and heard the rumbling of thunder, which before escaped his observation, so intent was he in his effort to capture the bird. "A hurricane for sure; I must find some kind of shelter until it is over."

Hardly had he made this resolution when the trees began to sway and bend as the oncoming wind tore its way among their branches accompanied by heavy clouds filled with rain, which soon began to pour down in torrents on the tree tops all about him. Within near reach of him was a fallen tree the trunk of which was raised by the upturned root, a foot or more above the ground. To this place he hastened and crawling under it, lay prone, sheltered from falling limbs and trees until the storm had wholly spent itself. When the storm was over he crawled out and began to cast about as to the way he would take to get back to the camp. The sense of direction, which to the Indian is a universal instinct, to Hector was a gift wholly lacking. In the midst of a thick forest with no hills nor rocks nor valley to guide him, only trees and all alike to him, there was nothing to aid his judgment as to the way by which he would rightly retrace his steps homeward.

He knew that he was not far from the shore of the bay, and if he reached this at any place, he would have no difficulty in finding the camp, if he would only again choose, when reaching there, the right direction. How many problems of our life would have had no existence for us, were the "ifs," which constantly pervade our future, only eliminated. Perhaps he was guided in his choice of direction by a desire to avoid the thickest woods, at any rate he chose that which provided the easiest and quickest way to travel in, and started out, determined to lose little time in getting back to the camp.

After he had walked a considerable distance, much farther than he had after the partridge, he observed that he was coming to a woods where the trees were mainly maples. Feverishly wishing that something would turn up, he was at last rewarded by coming to an Indian foot-path, which he knew would bring him in the water's edge somewhere. After following this for quite a lapse of time, it brought him to a hill on the brow of which was an Indian hut built for sugar-making purposes. On no occasion had any of the boys of the camp been at this place before, so that the discovery of the sugar-camp gave him no clue whatever, of the direction of the camp from these woods. He now began to realize the ugly possibility that he was lost, and as the night was fast approaching and the mist getting thicker, he would be well-advised to take shelter in this hut for the night. As he approached it, he observed it was made of cedar slabs, roofed with birch bark, and formed a neat and comfortable hut, well suited for the purpose for which it was made. Being square-shaped, he knew it to be the camp of an Objibway. On entering it, though getting dark, he was able to observe its inward appearance. The brass kettles for boiling the sap were neatly piled up in one corner; the hooks, made of wood, on which the Indians hung their sugar kettles over the fire, were moved to one end of the horizontal pole which stretched across the full length of the hut at the roof; the two raised platforms on either side, which had served the Indians for seats in the daytime and beds at night, had been covered with evergreen boughs over which had been laid mats, and still remained there as they had used them. Tired and wet, Hector, in this place of refuge, purposed he would spend the night.

Here at least was a shelter from the wind and rain, or rather the mist which now hung wet and thick over the surface of the whole island. A handsleigh, which had been used in the place of a door for the hut, Hector replaced and propped it up securely with a pole. Having finished these preparations, he sat down on the platform which was to provide him a bed for the night.

As so often happens in that north country, a sudden fall of temperature followed the rainstorms and Hector was beginning to feel the discomforting effects of the increasing cold.

"I wonder if there is anything around to build a fire," he thought.

Exploiting more minutely the contents of the hut, he discovered a flint set on a ledge above a bundle of cedars, and by its side a parcel tied up in a birch-bark covering which he judged to be the punk, the material employed by the Indians to catch the spark when lighting a fire. He put the flint in his pocket and began to examine the contents of the parcel. He discovered that instead of punk it was several small cakes of maple sugar which, in his foodless condition, he deemed to be a very fortunate discovery.

"I suppose it would be stealing to help myself to some of this, but for want of anything else to eat, I'll try one of them at any rate."

When he had eaten a couple, he put three others of them into his pocket.

"One each for the boys, and we'll instruct the Protector to discover the owner and restore him fourfold next spring."

This he deemed would be a sufficient concession to his own conscience and a satisfactory settlement with the Indian owners.

"Now for a fire," he observed as he continued his soliloquies, "which, thanks to our Indian friends, will not be a big job for they have everything here in readiness."

In a short while a cheerful blaze was affording him companionship and warmth, as he sat on the platform by its side and wished that the other three boys were there to share with him the experience of his adventure.

He was not destined, however, to spend the night alone. When but a short time seated, enjoying the light and heat from his newly-kindled fire, he was startled to immediate attention by hearing an animal come bounding toward the hut. Soon he heard the snuffling and scratching which it made in its effort to gain admittance. It did not take him long to come to an assured conclusion that this was none other than their pet Beagle, the mascot of the camp.

"The boys must have got back all right," he concluded, as she had been with them on their fishing excursion.

He rose up, and going to the door, opened a crevice and admitted his welcome visitor , who expressed her satisfaction in finding him by jumping and dancing about in mad glee, which ended by her nosing her head under his arm and taking her place seated by his side.

Just then his attention was attracted to another sound, interesting, but adding a tinge of loneliness to his situation. It was the beagle calls sounded, Hector well knew, to direct him homeward. His first impulse was to start out in another attempt to reach the camp, but he knew this would be to court an all-night exposure in the woods, and his better judgment told him, his comfort and safety lay in patiently remaining where he was.

"As soon as they are through, I'll give them an answer," he thought as he took hold of the gun and waited until the last note had died out of his hearing.

Going to the door he pointed the gun outward, having put on a fresh cap, and fired, yet the same result as before, but this time for an entirely different reason. The powder was damp, and Hector well knew that no amount of effort would enable him to send the message back to his companions, which he so earnestly desired to do.

After this incident Hector seated himself once more by the side of his fire, and began ruminating in his mind concerning the storm, his own misadventure, and the probable results which befell his companions' fishing excursion, nibbling as he meditated another of the Indian's cakes of maple sugar. It was not long, however, until through the kindly influence of the fire, he was heavy in sleep, stretched out on the Indian mat, and his little companion asleep also, lying close by his side

Once he was awakened through the night. The sudden drop of temperature added to his wet clothes, was producing an unfortunate after-consequence, influenza, and the chills of its approaching attack had awakened him up.

Late the next morning he awoke but it was to discover that his limbs were stiff and his skin burning with a fever heat. He made an effort to rise, but a whirring sensation passed through his head, and he was forced to lie down again. As he lay back in his weak and fevered condition on the mat, fortunately sleep again came to his rescue. How long this feverish slumber took possession of him he did not know, for day and night and length of time were being blotted out of his consciousness by his sickness.

When finally he received back some measure of his normal condition, and was capable of coherent thought, he began to put piece to piece together in his memory and by degrees realized that he had strayed away from the camp, that he was in a refuge hut, and that he would soon have to utilize his self to get back again.

He sat up, The gray dawn was beginning to creep through the crevices of the Indian Wigwam. He took down the sleigh, to enable the light to come through the open doorway. For want of any other food, he partook of a couple more of the cakes of sugar, and put all of the remaining ones into his pocket.

"It has taken away the feeling of hunger, at any rate, and perhaps after a while it will put strength and movement into my feet," he observed. "I think, however, I shall go out now and explore my whereabouts," was his next thought.

He stepped out into the open. The sun was just beginning to emerge above the eastern horizon, the air was cool and crisp, and the woods still wet from the effects of the rainfall and the subsequent heavy mist. Leaving the gun within the hut and the door open, he walked slowly down the trail, but in the opposite direction from which he came. Soon he arrived at an opening in the woods which led him to the waters of the bay. Approaching the shore, he observed lying before him a beautiful inlet gradually widening as it stretched itself outward to meet the main waters of the bay. Beyond, like a sheet of glass, were the waters of the Mer Douce, extending westward as far as his eyes could see.

It was a typical October day. Here and there were trees covered with crimson red, others a golden yellow, while the lighter green of the beeches, not yet discoloured, was overmatched by the deeper green of the firs, towering far above the rest. Near him was grove of silver birch, and Hector could see that this was a favourite Indian camping ground.

The plaintive cry of a loon on the far side of the inlet, and the gentle whine of the mascot at his side, added an eeriness to the place, which even the beauty of Nature could not take away.

Looking around, not more than five rods to his right, Hector observed two swarthy Indians sitting on the bank, eyeing him in silence and exchanging to each other no word of comment concerning his arrival. When he made as it were to approach them, they arose and went over to the beach where was their canoe. Hector noticed an empty bottle left where they had been sitting.

Behind their own, he now observed another canoe which at first was hidden from him.

What was his surprise to see that this was none other than the one that belonged to their camp.

"Where did you get that canoe?" he asked abruptly.

The young Indian rose up with a paddle in his hand and faced Hector.

"What you do here?" he answered angrily. "This Injun Reserve. You get off here."

"But that's our canoe," answered Hector back in that same peremptory tone of voice. "Where did you get it?"

The tone of his voice conveyed a different impression on the mind of the Indian than Hector intended. His questions were prompted by his desire to obtain knowledge of how the canoe came to be there, but the tone of voice produced by his surprise at seeing it there, led the Indian to believe that he was charging them with having pre-empted it. Unfortunately for Hector they were in that stage of intoxication which expresses itself in a quarrelsome mood, one of the worst effects of whiskey drinking upon all of their tribe. Without any warning, which might have led him to take some measure of defence or escape, the young Indian swung his paddle in the air with both hands and brought it down heavily upon Hector's head, felling him upon the ground, a senseless heap. The blow of itself was sufficient to produce this result, even if he had been in his normal condition, but Hector's weakness, due to his sickness, accentuated the probability of it, and prolonged the duration of its baneful effects.

The Beagle, seeing that her master was attacked, leaped at his assailant, and sunk her teeth into the calf of his left limb, but the second Indian came to his companion's assistance and soon beat the little animal into insensibility. Out of revenge for the mangling received by the dog, or perhaps thinking he was dead and wishing to leave no clue of his murderers, the Indians picked up the unconscious youth, carried him over and dumped him into his own canoe, and left him there stretched out prone on the bottom. Then towing the canoe a considerable distance out on the waters of the lake they cut it loose, and left Hector a helpless victim to the wind and waters of the bay, meeting any fate which Providence might measure out for him.

CHAPTER VII

AN HISTORIC SWORD:
AN HEIRLOOM AMONG THE OTTAWAS

In due time Hector came back to consciousness. Had he been in normal condition when the incident happened, the blow of the Indian would not have had so long an ill-effect upon him. As a consequence, when he made an effort to lift himself to a sitting position, a sharp pain shot through his head, the muscles of his body refused to answer to his will, a trembling sensation seized his body, and he was forced to remain for some time yet in the position where the Indians had placed him, lying at the bottom of the canoe. He had not sufficiently recovered to be able to follow out a train of coherent thought in respect to the circumstances in which he was now placed, nor had he enough of energy in purpose any settled aim or plan of activity. With a spirit subdued by his weakness and a will incapable of purpose, he left himself in the hands of a fate which he felt himself powerless to avert, stoically indifferent to whatever of consequences might follow. Kind Nature, however, again came to his rescue. The warm rays of the sun radiated obliquely upon him, warming his clothes, his body, and his blood, while the rocking of the canoe produced a sensation of comfortable repose, which was soon followed by a restful sleep taking complete possession of him.

When next he awoke the sun was shining down upon him from the mid-heavens, a measure of renewed strength had been given him, and he was able to effect a sitting posture on the bottom of the canoe. Scanning his surroundings to ascertain what possible future was in store for him, he descried all around him the blue waters of the Mer Douce, unbounded by the sight of any shore, its surface much troubled by a stiffening breeze blowing from the east.

Looking in the canoe to discover the usual equipment of paddles, he was greatly disappointed in finding that none were there. Either the boys had taken them out or they pre-empted by the Indians. But other equipment from the boys' fishing excursion were there—two duck, the gun and its ammunition, Rusty's great-coat, and a hand-axe.

"What more than that could anyone want, except for the paddles?" he commented as he examined them over one by one.

"Which way lies the mainland?" was the next problem which he made the subject of his meditations. He was inclined to the belief that it lay in the direction towards which the wind was blowing, but mindful of the errancy of his judgment concerning the points of the compass on a previous occasion, he hesitated to put too much faith in any conclusion based on his feelings alone.

"The prevailing wind is from the west and that would accord with my feelings, so," he concluded, "I must be drifting toward the mainland."

Thus reasoning, he judged that if the canoe kept on in the direction it was going it would soon reach land, either the mainland or some one of the many islands which were strewn along the full length of its shore.

"If I had only a paddle or anything to help myself," he thought aloud.

"Anything!" The mention of that word stirred his sluggish mind into activity. His body was still tired, his limbs stiff, and that ache in the head, though not so hard was still there.

"Anything!" he repeated, and looking around, his eyes rested on the gun.

"Why, there's a paddle, the stock a blade, and the barrel a handle; a paddle for sure," and he seized hold of it.

But this makeshift for a paddle was both too heavy and too clumsy to meet his approval so he placed it back again in its former position.

"We shall see what a sail will do instead," was his next thought.

He reached out and possessed himself of Rusty's coat. It was one of those in common use among fishermen and sailors of that north country—made of rough woolen material, woven in plaided colours and lined with tanned doeskin. Putting his hands through the sleeves backward, he took a central position in the canoe, adjusted himself in a sitting posture comfortably, and, facing the wind, spread it out before him. His improvised sail proved a complete success. The canoe sped over the waters, dipping and leaping, as the increasing gale carried it forward ahead at a rate that would have satisfied even a more exacting mind than that of Hector's. His spirit exhilarated with a thrill as he saw himself lifted once more to a position of self-helpfulness.

"At this rate, it matters little where 1 am," he soliloquized. "If I don't strike the one shore, I certainly will the other."

His enjoyment increased as he saw the canoe racing with the waves and outdistancing them. The seconds became minutes, and the minute hours, and yet there was no diminution in the pleasure which he was obtaining from the success of his experiment.

The afternoon was waning towards night, when surveying the sea before him, he discerned a dark shadow lying on the distant horizon. "An island or a cape," he concluded "but either one is welcome, for these waves are not getting any smaller."

His confidence that he would soon touch land became more buoyant as the shoreline of it continued to grow increasingly distinct every new time he scanned the waters before him. Yet the solution of one problem meant the raising of another'

"Will there be a landing? Or will it be a granite rock rising perpendicular from the shore, a foe to be feared rather than a friend be welcomed?"

This was the consideration now obtruding itself upon his mind with no little concern and anxiety.

As the canoe approached nearer, he observed that it was an island covered with a forest of evergreen and paper-birch trees. He directed the canoe to the right, purposing in swing around to the leeward and there seek a landing. He was led to this conclusion by the sight of gulls which he could see as dim specks rising up and flying about on the farther side of the forest of trees which separated them from him. Taking care not to approach too close to the shore so as to imperil his safety by the snow-capped waves, breaking themselves into huge columns of water, as they dashed against the rocky shore, he swung round the point, and soon found himself in safety on the sheltered side of the island.

He now observed that instead of one, he had come to a group of islands, the largest of which was covered with tall timber trees, but on the smaller ones, trees of stunted growth, the main varieties of which were cedar and jack pine. In the centre of the group there was a basin of water of probably five acres in extent. Here was found a sheltered spot not only for gulls and herons, but also for duck of various breeds and size, from the large mallard to the Diver, the latter, a duck, not only small in size, but its flesh worthless for human food. Hector also observed the ubiquitous loon sailing around among the other birds and, as usual, unaccompanied by any of its own kind. The islands of the group varied in size from a single boulder of granite rock, to one several hundreds of acres in extent.

Somewhere on this larger island Hector purposed he would select his camping ground for the night. Dispensing with his sail and using the gun for a paddle, he drew very close to the shore, that he might the better observe and discover a place of landing. The explorations were soon rewarded. A cove, cut into the rock, at the extremity of which he saw a sand beach slowly rising from the water, assured him that here was the most desirable of places to effect a. landing. The gulls, previously observed by him, were using this cove for a shelter. Some rose up noisily crying out their motley screams in protest against his uninvited intrusion, but others of them sat boldly still awaiting to see whether he should be classed as a friend or an enemy. Their presence gave to him a feeling of companionship he had not felt since the eventful evening, when his little pet, now dead, though he knew it not, found her way into the hut and took part with him in the series of misadventures, which had now reached their climax, by landing him alone on this far-off island.

He pushed his canoe forward until the bow rested on that more than welcome shore-line. Disembarking, for a moment he stood in the fresh waters with a thrill of pleasure, inspired by the thought that in the nick of time he had achieved his rescue from the dangerous possibilities which the increasing storm and the approaching night made doubly imminent.

He looked at the duck lying at the bottom of the canoe, and putting his hand in his pocket to assure himself that his flint and his knife were there, he spoke out: "Everything here for warmth and shelter. Luckily I put the flint in my pocket. I suppose that was stealing, according to a strict code, but when I get back I will square myself with the Indian and my conscience."

He drew his canoe far inland and deposited it within a grove of jack pines along side of which he immediately began the erection of a wigwam. A dead hemlock tree lay near with all its bark intact, although it had lain there for a number of years. With the aid of the axe, he began to bark this tree, and with care removed it off in large sections. In a short time he had a comfortable but erected, roofed and sided with this bark and this again covered with evergreen boughs, a double provision against the possibilities of wind, or rain, or snow, should any fall. With the same material, evergreen boughs, he made his bed for the night.

His next task was a fire, which, because of the fortunate discovery of the flint in the Indian wigwam, was an undertaking easy of attainment. This he lighted outside of the door of the hut proper, which enabled him to have the benefit of the heat and light inside, unattended by the discomfort of smoke. Over this he hung slices of duck flesh, and, as each piece was made edible, he ate slowly, but with relish; and sparingly also, remembering his long fast. By the time that he had finished cooking enough for his present need and some additional for the morning meal, he was quite ready to lie down in repose on his improvised bed of evergreen boughs. The lack of a blanket was made up by Rusty's mat. Buckling himself up in this blanket-like apparel, he lay listening to the hollow roar of the waves, as they dashed against the rock of the far shore of the island, and the wind, as it whistled dolorously among the branches of the tallest pines surrounding his hut, until sleep again overtook him.

The next morning he was early astir. His gray dawn was just beginning to chase sway the darkness of the night; the stars were still visible in the sky, but their light was appreciably growing dimmer. A dead calm reigned over the whole body of water. A more auspicious day for a canoeist could hardly be desired.

"I wish I had a paddle," was the first thought which took shape in his mind as he observed how suitable was the day for new adventures on the water. "But here's for something to eat first."

A heap of ashes lay where his fire had been burning the night before. Stirring this up, he found some coals still alive, and with the kindling which he had prepared the night before, soon had a glowing blaze wherewith he began the process of cooking the remaining part of his Mallard After finishing his morning meal he devoted himself to the making of a paddle with his jack-knife from a dried piece of cedar which he luckily found lying on the shore.

It was a long, laborious job, and seemed at first like an impossible achievement, but towards the close of the day, he was able to congratulate himself on its completion. The sun had gone down in a rainbow coloured sky. the presage of a good day for the morrow, and he was about to betake himself into his hut for the night when he was agreeably startled by hearing voices and seeing a canoe come round the point as himself had done the night before. When the occupants of the canoe had disembarked, they discovered themselves to be a Roman Catholic priest accompanied by two Indian guides. The priest was dressed in a black souture, one of those closely-fitting vestments commonly worn by the clergy of the Roman Catholic faith. He was a man above the average in both weight and height. His black beard was closely cropped and his hair also, over which he wore no covering. A large and round forehead, an aquiline nose, and a massive jaw gave the appearance of a strong personality. Hector rightly judged him to be French in nationality and in age about fifty years.

The presence of Hector, and alone at this lonely spot, was a matter of no little surprise in the new comers. The priest, the first to recover, smiled and saluted him in the French language.

Fortunately for Hector's upbringing and educational training, he was able to speak French fluently and therefore answered him back in his own tongue.

The priest came over and sat on the log which Hector, the night before, had stripped of its bark, and entering into conversation with him, observed, "You speak French; are you French?"

"No, but my father could speak it, and besides we were taught it in school. My father said he wanted me to learn it, for it was a language I would find of great service this country where there were so many people who could speak no other tongue. We had a French-Canadian servant, and our parents had her speak to us always in the French language. I think she must have been kept chiefly for that purpose."

Hector's ability to speak in the clergy-man's native tongue was an asset of great value to him on this occasion. It gave him a place in his sympathy and heart, which it needed only the narrative of his misadventure to make complete. He was not long in his presence when he received from him the information that he was a member of the Jesuit order, that his name was Marchand, and that he enjoyed the distinguished title of Monseigneur, given to him because of his fidelity and service on behalf of the Indians, a title of which, Hector observed, he was justly proud.

Hector in turn informed him of the events which transpired in his own little life during past few days and the anxiety with which he desired to get back to his companions.

"Your escape is miraculous. A miracle of grace, lad," the priest interposed as Hector narrated the event. "That is the only explanation; a miracle of grace. We shall have to seek some way now to get you back in safety."

"Are you going to camp here to-night?" Hector enquired, as he saw the Indians already making preparation to erect a. hut.

"Yes, we have come from the Detroit, and are visiting the Ottawas at Wilwemikongsing, on the south side of the Manitoulin, to-morrow."

"Are these Ottawas with you, Monseigneur?"

"Oh, no, these are Wyandots, or Hurons, from Bois Blane. They are part of the remnant who escaped from the Iroquois massacre in the middle of the 17th century. Some of them joined the Ottawas, but the most of them are at the Detroit."

"Is there an Indian village at Wikwemikongsing?" Hector further enquired.

"We are establishing one there. Houses have already been built, and we shall soon have a Mission established there. We have an industrial school for Indian children at Wikwemikong and a missionary in charge of it."

The Indians soon had their evening meal prepared, and Hector was invited to partake with them of the boiled pork, bread and tea, the usual fare provided for the priest when going the rounds of his Mission. Afterwards, both retired to Hector's hut, where, before the fire, the two sat for the whole evening, to mutual confidence, discussing many things but chiefly of the Indian and his destiny. "My People," as the priest affectionately called them.

"Do you know Little Knife, Monseigneur?" Hector enquired, wishing to hear more concerning this Indian of whom Rusty Brown had already told them much.

"Oh, yes; he often comes to our Mission."

"And Tehkummah and Assiginack?"

"Assiginack belongs to us; he has been baptized, but Tehkummah is a Pagan."

"But does baptism make any difference?" Hector asked, with sincere but unfeigned surprise.

Whether it was the question itself or the tone of surprise in Hector's voice, at any rate, he observed at once a change of countenance on the part of the priest which led Hector to believe he had struck a. discordant note.

"I mean," he continued in an attempt to right himself, "are they any better, is there any improvement, are they better morally and spiritually, because they have been baptized?"

Hector was not taking the attitude of a controversialist, but was seeking only to obtain knowledge of the power upon which this servant of The Cross was depending in order to bring about a transformation in the manners and morals of a race who had dwelt for centuries in the forest without any school of training save that of Nature. He had, however, raised a question which the priest himself had often puzzled over yet failed to find any satisfactory solution, other than that it was one of those mysteries we are called upon to believe yet not allowed to understand.

"It is the Lord's command, Hector," was his only answer. "We are to obey. It is God's work to give the power."

Hector proceeded no further in his questionings relative to a subject concerning which the wisdom of the ages have wrestled for centuries and yet so far have failed to find a basis for mutual faith fellowship. He was more interested in the people whom the missionary served than he was in church dogmas.

"In the war of the American Invasion, Assiginack was the chief of the Ottawas. I mean the Manitoulin Ottawas, was he not?" he asked.

"He was a brave warrior and had his men, but it was Little Knife who was their chiefest leader and most renowned warrior. They were recruited by a soldier of the American Revolution, Lieutenant MacLeod, who had a great influence over them, a dashing, fearless fellow, who trained them, and then led them into war."

The name at once aroused Hector's interest; its similarity to his own was apparently unnoticed by his clerical companion.

"Did he lead them in person?" he enquired.

"Oh, no, never, except when canoeing or planning an attack. They met in council. He gave them command what they should do, and then when they made a dash, left each man to his own devices. The Indians are best in a mob attack, and are invincible in a winning battle, but weaklings, if they have any forebodings of defeat. Lieutenant MacLeod, always inspired them as one who was bound to win and counseled them in such a way as to lead them to believe that they would surely win."

At this juncture, Hector rose up and added more fuel to his fire, for the night was chill, and they needed the comfort of its warmth as well as the companionship of its cheerful blaze.

Lieutenant MacLeod was a very determined man," began the Monseigneur, when Hector was again seated. "Once, when he started out with his men from Penetanguishene with flour and pork for the Fort, and the garrison were sore in need of provisions, they were caught in a great storm on the East Shore Islands. I was with them. They had one sailboat and two canoes. I was in one of the canoes; Lieutenant MacLeod was in the sailboat. In the morning, I said to him, "There is coming on a storm, Lieutenant, and here is a good place for us to stay until it is over.' But he was determined he would go on, storm or no storm."

"We must push on, Monseigneur," he answered; "go until we can go no further. We have a long journey yet before us, and the men are hungry at the fort."

"'If we face that storm'," I said, and I could see it coming on "'We'll not go any further, but we'll drown'."

" 'Whatever men dare they can do. That is the song of the Camerons, and though we haven't got their blood, we must have their spirit,' he answered with determination."

" 'No, no, Lieutenant, it is not that, but whatever men can do, they can dare,' I explained to him. 'The fool can dare, but he can't do everything he dares. If he could, then the wise man is the fool and the fool is the wise man. The Apostle Paul was a wise man, and he could dare. There never was a Cameron that had a braver heart and a more willing mind. The things great men feared, he counted them as refuse; but there was One up there, and when he said 'Thou shalt not,' he could not. No, no, Lieutenant, 'Thou shalt not tempt the Lord thy God'."

"You may be right, Monseigneur," he answered "but the sail-boat will have to face the storm." To the men he said, "Unload the canoes, draw them out of the water." To me he said, "Stay here until you feel safe to go further, but the sail-boat will have to keep going on."

" And go they did, Lieutenant MacLeod, Little Knife, Dupuis and Devine. That day

And that night there was a storm, never there was a storm, never a worse one before on the lake. Three days after before we started. We passed one group of islands and were going past another when we heard someone shout, and there was Dupuis and Devine standing on the shore and waving at us. We went over. The sailboat was lying upon its side capsized in shallow water. MacLeod and Little Knife and the young warriors were off. They saved the flour and the pork and were away with it for the Fort in canoes, They reached it—three hundred and sixty miles—but it took them three weeks. When they arrived the flour of the garrison was done, their pork was done and the soldiers on half rations of venison and fish which the Indians had brought them."

"And the sail-boat was lost?" enquired Hector.

"Oh no, they came back, built rafts, and windlassed it to the surface again."

"You say it was Little Knife who was presented with the silver-mounted sword for having saved the American officer from being scalped when he brought him into the Fort to the commandant, wounded?"

"Yes, that was the Indian, the same as was with Lieutenant MacLeod, and he was fighting with the Lieutenant when it happened. The officer his name was Reinhardt, he belonged then to the Americans but in the Revolutionary War, he was an Hessian."

At this the priest ceased his narrative. A pained look, as of a memory dwelling on unpleasant thoughts, came over his countenance. After a time he looked again towards Hector.

"This Hessian, I think, was known by Lieutenant MacLeod in the American War."

"Was Lieutenant MacLeod present when Little Knife received the sword?"

"Oh yes, for it was he who told the commandant and recommended it. Yet something happened afterward. Rheinhardt was a Catholic, and I administered to him and made many prayers and his behalf and he got better. Twice his life had been saved. A bullet went through his face, and there was a scar on each cheek. When he was better and gone, I told this one day to Lieutenant MacLeod, and he jumped up with the rage of a tiger. I never saw a man that angry before. And then he sat down calm and pale, and said to me, as a man speaking the words of another, "The Avenger of Blood must be the Next of Kin',"

"What did he mean?"

"I don't know. There was a look in his face that made my blood cold. 'Monseigneur,' he said to me, 'you were right about the storm. If I dared to do what I want to do, there. would be murder. I am trying to live one way, but there are two others trying to make me live another—to use me, to guide me, and to govern me. One would have me break my promise, and kill one who ought not to live, but whom the good God seems to want to protect. That is the person which my will wants to follow. And there is yet another and it says, 'Thou shalt not.' As Barak was helpless, blessing those whom he did not want to bless, and cursing those whom he was paid to bless, so the man whom I would kill, I have taught my Indians to save; and the man who has robbed me of love and home, I protect, and only because, that person says, 'Thou shalt not'."

"'Father Marchand,' he said, giving me my first title, the one he knew me by before I was made Monseigneur, 'I want you to pray for me; pray for me always,' and he went out from my presence like a man demented."

"When is 'shedding of blood' justice, Monseigneur, and when is it murder?" Hector interrogated.

"I don't know. Sometimes we call Justice, murder; and murder, Justice." Again, the priest lapsed into silence, with the same pained look over his face.

"Was Lieutenant MacLeod a Catholic?" asked Hector, somewhat hesitatingly.

"No," answered the faithful servant of that ancient and honourable church, "but I think he was a good man, greatly tempted."

"You still pray for him, Monseigneur?"

"I prayed then, that he might be kept from murder, and for that I shall pray for him always."

"Have you seen Lieutenant MacLeod there?"

"Not in the flesh; but every night at this time of the year, but a little later, his spirit stands before me, and just as the sun goes down, the same look, the same voice, and this is what it says; "The land cannot be cleansed of the blood that is shed therein but by the blood of him that shed it'—and then I pray, and I cannot but pray, that his hand may be stayed from the shedding of that blood, which he would, but must not, shed."

"The spirits of the departed, suppose you, Monseigneur, that they appear again on the earth?"

"We must believe, mon petit gareon, what we experience."

The night was now far spent. The breathing of the two Indians in the near-by tent where they lay in deep sleep, could be distinctly heard.

The priest passed over one blanket to Hector; the other, he folded about his own body and stretched himself out on the bank of evergreens bough prepared for him. Soon the deep breathings of Monseigneur Marchand were heard by Hector informing him that he too had followed the Indians into the land of forgetful sleep.

But Hector lay awake, thinking of lieutenant MacLeod, his grandfather, and his vague hints of a tragedy in the army, was this his lost uncle, a. glimpse into whose life this wandering servant of the Cross had permitted him to see. Was he dead? He must be since he disappeared from one, who, by his numerous travels, could have kept trace of him better than any other could. If , too, the seance of Monseigneur Marchand's faith had reality in material fact, then it could only be because he too had gone the way of all men. And then Hector turned in thought to Parry Island, to Rusty Brown and his companions, until after long wakeful meditation on the enigma, of life, he went asleep conscious of a comradeship in events leading him in ways whether he would not go, but must.

CHAPTER VIII

A DEFERRED HOPE

The priest was early astir and had the Indians ready for the return journey to the Detroit with the break of day. Out of respect for Hector, contrary to their usual custom of making a part of their journey before partaking of their morning meal, Monseigneur Marchand had ordered breakfast to be got in early readiness. While this was in process of preparation both strolled as the western point of the island in order that Hector might have accurate information of the location of Wikwernikong, the village of the Ottawas, to which he was being directed by the priest.

The golden sun had arisen up in a cloudless sky and was throwing down its effulgent rays on the silvery forest of the Great Mantoulin, lying in visible outline to the westward before them. The cool crisp air of the early October morning, the forecast of a premature winter, produced a tingling sensation not at all uncomfortable, but rather bracing. A heavy white frost had fallen through the night and every tree was enrobed in a dress of whiteness, giving to the eye the appearance of a snow-covered forest. A dead calm lay over the whole body of the water which separated their island from this Indian village.

"It will only take you a short half-hour to reach it," the priest informed Hector. "You will find Nekig there, who is going to return to his home to the Parry Island village to-morrow and you will have his company all the way back."

Hector was jubilant at the fortunate turn of events which would not only enable him to return to Parry Island, but accompanied, as the priest assured him, with one who was intimately acquainted with Rusty Brown, and would be ready to serve him for his sake if for no other.

The two canoes pulled out together, the priest and his Indians directing theirs southward, but Hector westward towards the isle of the Great Spirit. After they had made some little distance out on the water they waved each other adieu with their paddles, and Hector was left once more alone to try out new ventures on the waters which separated him from his companions.

As he drew near the Manitoulin coast he observed at the far end of the bay, a village of about forty houses set on the brow of the hill, and stretching in irregular line all around the shore. When he arrived, he observed in addition to these Indian dwellings, and set some distance behind the village proper, a building in process of construction, the Mission House mentioned by the priest which was intended to be used for both school and church purposes. In the erection of this building a large number of Indians were engaged. One was splitting shingles with a frow from cedar blocks while two others were smoothing these with drawing-knives. Four axe-men were on the building shaping the ends of the logs, and adjusting then into neat and well-fitting dove-tailed grooves, a method of carpentry or axemanship taught the Indians by the early French, and in which, being apt scholars, they became very expert. A score or more were employed in falling trees and carrying the logs by hand to the building. A final group, principally old men, were lounging around, employing themselves as spectators of the others doing the work.

Hector made his way to this scene of activity and on arriving within hearing distance accosted them with the usual salutation of these regions, "B'shoo, B'shoo."

He was answered with a chorus of "B'shoos."

The corner-men ceased their work, and one inquired of him in very good English, "You a trader?"

"No," answered Hector, addressing his remarks to the young man on the corner who spoke to him. "I have lost my way and I want to get back to Parry Island."

"Parry Island a long way from here; lots of miles from here."

"Could I get there to-day?"

"May-be and may-be not; depends on that and how fast you paddle."

"In what direction is it from here?"

The Indian pointed north-eastward.

"Can you tell me where is Nekig?"

The Indian addressed turned to a young lad standing near, attracted to the place by the sight of Hector. This youth turned and ran to a neighbouring house, and soon there emerged a girl about sixteen years of age. When she came over, Hector observed she had fair hair and blue eyes, but otherwise differed in no respect from any other of the Indian girls of her age. The elder Indian spoke to her in her own language, and soon there was a general conversation carried on in the Indian language, the purport of which Hector could not understand. Remembering the service rendered by his knowledge of the French the night before with the priest, he spoke to the young girl in that language, and was rewarded in finding one who, educated in a Montreal girls' school, could speak it with equal fluency.

"Could you tell me where may I find Nekig?" he asked her.

"Down on the shore, there miles across at the Cave of the Spirit," was her answer.

"Is he going to the Parry Harbour village to-morrow?"

"That's where he lives."

"Do you know him?"

"Yes, he's my uncle."

"Do you live with him?"

"No, I live with my grandmother."

"Is your mother there, too?"

"No, my mother is dead."

"And the missionary, is he anywhere around?"

"No, he went just a few minutes ago to Wikwemikongsing."

"Gone there to meet Monseigneur Marchand, I suppose. What's his name?"

"Kohler. He wants all Indians to live and no white folks."

"Do the Indians want that, too?"

"Some Indians sign the paper to sell the island to the white folks, but other Indians say 'No,' This is a big island, one hundred miles long, full of lakes and fish and beaver, and they want no white folks here."

"Do you suppose I could get Nekig to go to Parry Island with me to-day?"

"Perhaps, if he was here."

"Do you think any of these men would go with me?"

In answer the girl turned to the Indians, now sitting around idle, some smoking pipes, others listening, taking heed to the conversation, as a considerable number of them were capable of speaking the French language, and more of them understanding it. When she informed them of Hector's request, a jabber of tongues began among them as before, and Hector surmised, as it continued for some considerable time, that the girl warn interpreting all of their conversation to them.

"Kish-ke-nick says he'll take you to Parry Island if you have something," she informed him after a while.

This "something" might mean wages, or more likely the commodities with which the traders obtained service from the Indians of which rum and brandy were the first in importance. It was doubtless this which the Indian had in mind when he asked if he had something. But as Hector knew nothing about the value set by an Indian on this commodity, he answered that he had only with him the gun and ammunition, the fishing tackle which, with Rusty's coat, comprised all the equipment of the canoe. He would give him readily anything he wanted when he got back to their camp if he would undertake to guide him there. Having thus expressed his willingness to pay for any service rendered him, he enquired of the girl.

"Which one is Kish-ke-nick?"

She pointed to the young man who had first spoken to him. Hector observed now, what escaped his attention before, that the young man had only three fingers on his left hand, the forefinger having been dismembered by an accident when a boy, and hence his name, the significance of which was "cut hand."

At the invitation of Hector they both, followed by some of the others, walked down in the shore where his canoe was beached. On their arrival there, Hector pointed out the equipment of his comrades lying at the bottom of the canoe. The gun attracted the notice of the Indian immediately. Seeing this, Hector took it up and placed it in his hands.

"Me shoot?' said the Indian, requesting its privilege of testing the value of the fieldpiece.

"Why most certainly," answered Hector, Readily and taking the powder-horn and shot-pouch handed both to him.

The Indian stalked down the shore towards a cove in the bay where a flock of duck were sheltering themselves. For half an hour he remained away. Two shots were heard, fired off in the interval. When Kish-ke-nick appeared afterwards, his face was illuminated by a broad smile. He carried six duck in his one hand and the fieldpiece in the other. Resting the gun on its stock, and with apparent and eager desire to own it, he said to Hector when he reached his presence, "Give it me; me take you to Parry Island."

"I will gladly give it to you," said in answer to his request, "if you take me back there to-day."

The Indian assented at once and began immediate preparation for their journey. Hector was delighted at this fortunate turn in the events of his journey.

"It will not be long now until the boys'll see my shadow approach the door of the camp," he meditated to himself, "I'll give them the surprise of their life, if not to-night then to-morrow at any rate, when they see me coming round the point into the bay with their canoe."

So hopeful was Hector of the sure outcome of their journey, that he deemed himself almost already there. He did not consider that three-quarters of the whole width of the Mer Douce lay between his point of starting on his journey and the place of ending it. With the gift of hope, the greatest asset to the happiness of the human race, Hector was generously endowed by nature. The word was written deeply and legibly on his forehead. The clearer the word is written, the less fear and trembling doubt there is in life; but the dimmer the writing the more easily does the spirit give way to despair. Optimism was Hector's outstanding native gift. In addition to the liberal endowment of this native gift, he also was blessed with another very important trait of character. Like the race to which he belonged, he was gifted with a mind of determined purpose. It would take a large task to turn him away through fear of failure from venturing on its accomplishment. His desire to hire an Indian guide was to hasten the accomplishment of his journey rather than to increase its safety. He had no fears as to its ultimate issue. Impatient to begin his journey, he appreciated the quick return of Kish—ke-nick carrying two well-shaped new paddles in his hand.

"I thank you heartily for those paddles, Kish-ke-nick. They certainly are two dandies. When shall we make the start?"

Kish-ke-nick made no vocal reply, but smiled the part which he felt in seeing Hector in so animated and cheerful a spirit, and going over to the canoe began to push it out into the water.

A squaw, apparently his mother, appeared with the provisions and equipment for the journey, and placed them in the centre of the canoe. Hector took his place at the bow with Kish-ke-nick at the stern, and both putting their paddles into the water at the same time the canoe was turned northward, and started out on its journey to the main land. Groups of the villagers, some standing on the shore, others sitting on the brow of the hill, watched the canoe embark on its journey and continued interested spectators until it, and its two occupants, had passed out of their sight.

Hector and his companion paddled together strongly. They skirted along the eastern shore of the Manitoulin, crossing Manitowing Bay at its junction with the Mer Douce in short time, and then still northward until they came to Sheguiandah Bay. Here was another Indian village, an encampment of about a dozen families of the Ojibway tribe.

These had not yet reached the stage of progress attained by the Ottawas at Wikwemikong. They were all housed in wigwams, some of which were made of cedar slabs, carefully split thin, and overlapping each other, while others of them were made of cedar bark. These were arranged in the usual manner of Indian villages in semi-circular shape with the guest wigwam of the chief occupying a central position. Kish-ke-nick was apparently acquainted with the place and its residents. Making his way to his dwelling, which he knew by its larger size, the chief soon appeared and led Hector to the guest wigwam. Here he was plentifully regaled with a supper of hominy and venison. The usual platforms were covered with a half-dozen or more of bear skins, which bespoke a comfortable bed for their night's rest.

Kish-ke-nick went out after supper with the chief and did not again appear until after daylight the following morning.

In the interval he had fallen in with a party of hunters who were on their way to the La Cloche region, an incident which led to the miscarriage of Hector's expectations to have this Indian safely guide him back to their encampment on Parry Island. Indians are always Indians, changeable, and moody, the willing servants of caprice and momentary impulse. The glowing accounts which the hunting party gave of the favourable prospects for game, at a place where herds of deer were recently seen assembled, induced Kish-ke-nick to join this party.

This purpose was not made known to him until they had reached the mainland of the north shore, when he was given the option to either to accompany the Indians on their hunt, returning in the course of a few days or to venture alone the rest of the journey to Parry Island. He had no hesitation in choosing the latter alternative.

CHAPTER IX

MAROONED

When Hector found himself so unexpectedly forsaken by his guide, he began to realize that it was imperative that he should not delay in pushing forward towards his destination. His gun was gone; so also the fishing tackle. The Indian had received these in payment for a service which he had not rendered. These he would not need if were no mishaps to prevent the immediate completion of his journey. Should there be unexpected delay, then the want of these to provide for himself food would be sorely felt.

As we have observed, inactivity or despair were alien to his nature. When the hunting party had turned westward, and Kish-ke-nick no longer with him, he took his place in the centre of the canoe and began energetically to paddle his way forward in the opposite direction. The day was yet young and there were many hours of daylight still before him

His course led him through groups of islands which strewed the shore practically along the whole length of his journey. Occasionally he had some difficulty in finding his way among these, which retarded in some measure his rate of speed. He was making satisfactory progress until, winding along a group of islands, he felt something graze the bottom of the canoe. It was one of those submerged islets of granite rock which appear and disappear with every rise and fall of the level of the lake.

"I shall have to watch more carefully when going through places like this," he said to himself.

In a few moments after, to his amazement, he saw water oozing through a hole in the bottom of the canoe.

"I must beach her and see if I cannot stop that hole-somehow.

He was now half-way between two islets and made for the nearest. It was only a short distance so he felt assured he could reach it, but unfortunately the water kept coming in more rapidly, an evidence that the rent in the bark of his canoe was getting larger. He realized to his sorrow that there was nothing to do but to abandon it and swim the rest of the distance between him and the shore. It was doubtless the abuse which was given to the canoe as it drifted from the time it got away from the boys which caused the slight corrosion which the grating off the rough surface or the jagged edge of the submerged rock to tear so great a hole in it. But at any rate Hector found himself marooned on this island without food or shelter or any way of escape unless some vessel should chance to pass by.

At first he felt like giving away to a spirit of disappointment, almost akin to despair. But he was too alert and active to sit brooding over his misfortunes in idleness. The island on which he was landed was devoid of trees or shelter of any kind, but another a short distance away was well wooded.

"I shall have to make for the shelter of those trees," he said to himself, "If I am to stay here very long."

Divesting himself of his clothes and making a bundle of them, he strapped these with his suspenders on the back of his shoulders. The distance was short, the water smooth and quiet, and it was not long until he was safely landed on this more advantageous rock.

"Here I can have a fire, at any rate," he spoke aloud, as he stood up on the shore, "if so be that I have not lost my flint and knife coming across."

He fished them out of the now soaking pocket in which he had carried them.

"Here they are all right. Now for a fire and a dry-up, but nothing to eat, and I am getting hungry already."

Ringing out his clothes, he spread them out on the rock to dry.

The sun shone down through the dry October air, and created such a warmth, that it was not long until Hector was re-clothed in civilization's garb, his clothes showing no traces of the two water voyages they had made that morning.

"I will never leave thee, nor forsake thee," the priest, Monseigneur Marchand, had quoted for his encouragement. Hector repeated the words over to himself to strengthen his fortitude and hope.

"Well, I'm not drowned anyway, and that is a blessing which ought to make me thankful all the rest of my life, if so be I can get away from this place before I starve to death."

As Hector explored round about the shore in search of a place to build a fire, best observed by a passing vessel on the bay, his interest was attracted to a channel cut into the island, at the end of which he discovered a cave of considerable dimensions. He crept through the opening that led into this cave, and from a beam of light that shone down through the narrow crevice from the top towards the back of the cavern, he was able to make a complete survey of the whole interior.

"What's this?" he said, as, standing up, he looked over a ledge revealing to him a second apartment, separated from the first lay a wall of rock over which he was now looking "Somebody's cache! What a lucky discovery."

He lifted himself over his wall of rock and began making minute inspection of everything stored away in this unexpected spot cans and bottles and boxes, some blankets and a revolver loaded ready for action. The bottles he ascertained to be filled with intoxicating liquors, and the boxes with food. Hector was puzzled. Was this the chance discovery of a. long-forgotten cache? There was no sign round about as if it were a frequented spot. Indeed every evidence seemed to indicate that the place had been unvisited not merely for weeks but months. Hector examined one box to find that it was filled with sea biscuits or "hard tack," as they are more usually named.

"Whoever owns it, certainly it is a. lucky me, that they are here if I'm to be marooned very long at this place."

The gay-spirited laugh, that used to fill the camp at Parry Island with cheer, echoed inside the cavern, but stillness gave it such an uncanny sound that Hector, in spite of the pleasure aroused in finding the food, felt himself seized with a nameless awe which he could not dispel till he again went out and walked the shore, wondering at the significance of the cave and its contents. The presence of intoxicating liquors in such quantities caused him to conclude, and that rightly, that this was the storehouse of some Indian trader—that class of men who once frequented the bay in great numbers, intent only for the sake of its gain, of spreading debauch among the aboriginal inhabitants of the country.

Taking a. handful of the biscuits with him, he sat down on the shore and began eating them slowly and with a pleasure which was enhanced by the background of assurance, that, with such a store of pro visions, a long day would intervene before starvation would be a calamity which he would need to fear.

Roaming about, he made a still more unexpected though gruesome discovery. On a spot of shallow ground a little distance from the cave, he observed a hollow, at the end of which he saw the foot of a skeleton protruding: The soil was soft and mellow, and was easily removed with the hand. Heater busied himself now in unearthing what proved to be the complete skeleton of a man, with every part intact, save that the skull was fractures as evidence of foul play as the cause of his death. The major part of the afternoon he spent in reconstructing the skeleton, putting each part in its own place, until he had the completed form lying out on the ground before him.

"Perhaps," he thought, "it is the owner of the cache. Poor fellow, but who could have buried him?

After this Hector again took his seat on the shore, looking seaward in hope that some vessel or canoe might come within observation of him; but it was one of the most unfrequented waters of the bay. The Indian trader had chosen wisely the place of concealment for his illicit commodity. As he sat there, his thought went back to Pleasant island, the missionary, his message to the Indians, their hymns and their prayers. He recalled also his own favourite:

"I have anchored my Hope in my Haven of rest; I shall fear the wild surf no more; the billows may sweep, O'er the storm-tossed deep, But through Him, I am saved evermore."

He turned the hymn over and over again in his mind, meditated upon its meaning, to find his thought rise up in expectant hope to one who Himself knew the deep meaning of Loneliness, but never of Despair. The reveries of Hector made him oblivious to all passing circumstances, and blotted out all sense of time. He looked up; the sun had set. A grayness was hanging over the waters that was fast hastening to become the blackness of night. A deep stillness prevailed. A mystic solemnity, an awesome courage, possessed his spirit. The night had become chill. Hector bethought himself of the blankets. He lighted a little fire in the cavern, with prepared material, and under the light of its cheering blaze, he made himself a tolerably comfortable place to rest. He viewed the gum—it was rusted and worthless, but the knife, it was unrusted and intact. He set it by his side, for it seemed to him a companionable friend in the darkness of the night. The comfort of the blankets and the warmth of the fire, soon provided a deep sleep which made him unconscious of the night and its dangers.

But through the night his slumbers were rudely disturbed by hearing human voices and .the dip of paddles not far from the mouth of the cavern.

As the men approached he listened to their conversation.

"It's seven years, Jacques."

"Ay, ay, it's seven years now to the very day. I wish it were the day instead of the night we'd come."

"I suppose ye're afraid of Magrigger's ghost."

"Poor Magrigger! I can see his poor pitiful face, and his words I can hear them every night since, "For God's sake, if you have any soul, think of my wife and my little boy!"

"Ay, ay. Rheinhardt was the hardhearted cuss. A man that'd sell the soul of an Indian for an extra dollar was not the stuff to mind a cry of a fatherless bairn."

"And how he laughed when he said, 'I didn't want to finish the two Frenchies. but a dead men tell no tales'."

"Do you think the Frenchies knew?"

"If they had eyes, they certainly did, for either of them was as drunk as Rheinhardt appeared."

"Do you think they would have told?"

"Told! Certainly! A Frenchie has never been known to keep a still tongue in his head. Forby, if MacKenzie would get to know he would be right on our tracks, and he would follow us and watch us like a cat. You might keep out of the road of an Indian, but not of Rory MacKenzie, if he makes up his mind to find you. But have ye the torch, man?"

"Right here in my hand!"

"And the flint?"

In answer he pulled the steel and flint out of his pocket and began to strike fire, but after getting started, for some unaccountable reason, the fire went out.

"Tut, tut, didn't know there was so much wind."

"It must be rising. But hurry up and let's get out of here, for it's not myself that wants to be here long at this time of night."

"Tut, tut, another gone out."

"Another? Then it's not the wind, but an unholy spirit of the dark, or I've not been taught truth at my mother's knee."

"There's another."

"Another, that's three. Then it's Magrigger, for his bones must be somewhere near here, and his spirit will be back to the old place to-night. My mother used to tell that they came back every year and it's just as like he'll be back to-night."

"Here we go this time." And the torch flickered out its guiding flame over the water.

The men moved to the cavern approaching. Hector could clearly observe them. One was a short, stout man with dark, bushy hair; the other, tall and thin. Both had whiskers over their face and of the same dark colour as their hair. They looked the part of the trade they followed.

Hector reached out, and took hold of the rusted, useless gun found in the cavern, just as they reached the entrance, and rose up in a half-standing posture, with the weapon in his hand.

For a second both of the men stood and stared. It seemed to Hector like an age, so still was the moment and his spirit. He pushed his hand as if to aim at one, or both. The motion aroused the taller from the stupor of fear which the unexpected sight of Hector had at once produced. Without a word he turned and ran. The shorter one, and with the torch, followed quickly, but in doing so stumbled over the bones of McGregor, now laid out on the ground in natural shape by Hector. With a yell he dropped the torch and fled with greater haste. When they reached the canoe, he heard a third man.

"What now, what now," and with an oath, "You fools?"

"Holy Ghosts! The cave is full of them. They've got you at last Rheinhardt!"

"Jump in ye cowards and get out of here!"

Immediately they pushed from the shore and were out on the water.

Hearing their hurried departure and the rapid dipping of their paddles in the water, Hector breathed more freely. The instinct of preservation, or involuntary courage, of a divine inspiration, moved him to quick action. He seized the torch and put it out.

"Ay, they know their business! Out goes the light!" Hector heard coming back from over the water, for already they had put much distance between and the shore.

Hector was now too unnerved to go back to the cave. His heart beat rapidly, his body trembled from head to foot. The meaning of the skeleton had now been made known to him. It was a murder, and he was standing enveloped in darkness in the place where the villainous deed had been done.

That the participants of the deed hesitated to go back to the place of crime was evident since they kept away from it for so long, and even now visited it, as their conversation disclosed, very
reluctantly.

Hector's heart continued in a state of flutter, "I wish I hadn't put out the light after all; if I had it I could see to get back to the cave." But soon to his great relief he could see the lifting of the darkness in the east. With the thought that the daylight would soon be with him, he went into the cave. He stirred up the ashes of the night fire and found there a smoldering ember which he soon blew into a little blaze. In short time the cave was lit up with its companionable light, and with the aid of one of the burning embers, he built another fire on the shore. He was not now afraid of the arrival of the three visitors of the night, but hoped that ere long he might attract the attention of some passing craft.

The darkness that lay as a blanket over the blue waters of the Mer Douce, now lying in placid calm, was being gradually lifted up, supplanted by the grayness of the approaching morn. At this juncture, Hector was gladdened at the sight of a canoe, bearing directly on the island and with three persons in it. As soon as they neared the shore, he observed that they were three Indians.

After their landing, an animated conversation followed, conducted in the Ojibway language. Hector understood nothing of their conversation, but he had reason to that he was the subject of it. The Indians in the meantime, prepared him a breakfast of fresh fish, bread and tea, and showed him no little kindness, after which the younger of the three informed him in good English that they were on a canoe trip, which they must first finish, after which they would come back and take him with them.

Hector protested, but Indians are all alike they'll do the thing you want, but only after it pleases them.

"You surely do not intend to leave me here alone. Your canoe can stand four persons. Why not let me go along with you?"

"We not going far. Be back soon."

"How much money do you want to take me to Parry Island? Name it now, and I'll give it to you when I get there."

"We come back after a little. You all right. We come back soon, sure."

Away from this attitude of mind Hector could not wean them. As a matter of fact, these Indians were out for the express purpose of finding him. They knew of the large reward that was offered for his discovery by Rusty Brown. They were delighted in the flick that enabled them to find him, but desired the assurance from Rusty, that it would be paid to them before bringing him with them from the island. Indian-like, they did not know that he might not be there when they returned, so unable are they to reason out a problem to its legitimate conclusion.

As the Indians paddled away, the younger of them waved back his hand.

"We'll be back after a while," he heard him say by way of further assurance that his rescue from the island was a coming certainty.

The solitude of the island would have been less discomforting if the whiskey-traders, in the unexpected hours of the night had not put in an appearance.

"To think that they took me for the spirit of the departed dead," thought Hector, and laughed aloud as he remembered their fear.

After the Indians were out of sight, he sat down by the fire on the shore, and took out a Latin Bible, with which the missionary had equipped him, and began reading it. Commencing at the beginning, he read on, chapter after chapter and book after book, stopping once in a while to put some more fuel on the fire. This reading he kept up at intervals throughout the day, an exercise which not only supplied him with pastime, but also fortified him with a courageous hope that a safe ending would issue out of his misadventures.

CHAPTER X

A COMPLICATED DRAMA OF FRONTIER LIFE

The day was beginning to wane towards evening, when looking southward, Hector descried on the distant horizon the sail of an approaching schooner. As it came northward he observed it was not passing too far from the direction of his island, but that he might be able to signal it to come to his rescue. He began at once to take measures with that end in view. He recreated his fire on the shore, erected a pole at the end of which he attached a handkerchief as a flag of distress, and improvised a megaphone, made out of bark which earlier in the day he had picked off a neighbouring silver-birch. When the sail got directly opposite him, he called out through it to attract their attention. His efforts were immediately rewarded.

What do you want?" shouted back a voice apparently that of the captain of the schooner, who had come over to the side of the vessel.

"Can you land and take me with you? I'm stranded on this island and no way to get off," Hector answered, still using his megaphone.

Immediately the schooner was steered shoreward, and the sails reefed. A dinghy, towed behind, was unloosed from the vessel, entered into by the man who had spoken to him, and sculled over to the beach where Hector stood.

"Hello, there, boy, how many are there of you?" he asked, when he got within speaking distance.

"Only myself," answered Hector, "I had a mishap with my canoe yesterday, and so had to swim here for safety."

"And you here since, eh, and no one to see you?"

"Some Indians were here this morning but they went away saying they would come for me later."

"Come later, eh? You can't depend on an Injun for nuthin'. And where do you want to go now?

"Parry Island or the Indian Village. My friends are at Parry Island, but I can get there easily from the village."

"I can take you to the La Cloche to-night and day after to-morrow I'll drop you off at the village on my way back."

"Can't you take me to the village tonight? My people will make it more profitable to you than going to the La Cloche."

"Not to-night, boy. I have orders to be there to-night and it would put me out of the way, but I can sail in coming back and lose no time. It's the orders, boy, and I can't go 'gainst orders."

"But I have been away now nearly a week, and my friends will think me either dead in the woods, or drowned."

"A week! Is that all, boy? I've been away now over a month from my folks, and I'll do well if I see them again before the season's close. One day more is neither here nor there. You can come along with us and be at the village to-morrow, or the day after to-morrow, or you can take chances on the Injuns paddling you over to their village next week."

Then looking around and apparently scanning the darkening waters to see if there were any signs of canoes, he continued:

"Boy, you're lucky that we're here. I never come this way, nor does anyone else except Injuns, and I'm here only because I wanted a short cut to La Cloche."

Flourishing an oar as if preparatory to sculling back, "Come along, boy," he impatiently commanded, "get your belongings and let us hike out of here."

"My belongings are on my back, sir,"

"All better, then; you'll weigh less and take up less room on the craft."

"Wait, I've got something here I want to take with me," requested Hector, as he thought of the skeleton bones. He had carefully placed this discovery in a birch-bark basket found in the cache, and had them all in readiness for removal, when it would be his luck to be taken off the island. The basket lay at the mouth of the cache, and Hector went thither to pick it up. The Captain attracted the appearance of the cavity of the rock towards which he saw Hector making, jumped out of the boat and followed after him.

"What have we got here?" he exclaimed, as he came up to it.

Keenly curious, he went in as Hector did before him, stumbling along on the ledge of the rock until he reached the sand bottom at the further end of the channel. Then looking over the rock, a loud laugh served to inform Hector, without, that the discovery of what lay about and before his eyes was a surprise delightful to the Captain.

"Magrigger's cache!" he exclaimed, as he discovered the goods of the trader's traffic.

This was followed by another laugh as he saw numerous cases of trader's goods and bottles filled with intoxicating liquors stored away in this secluded place, and bearing evidence of being a long time here untouched.

Emerging from the cave, he remarked, "Boy, you are the first person to see this cache in six years."

"Two men were here last night," replied Hector.

"They were! And what did they do?"

"When they saw me in the cave, they ran away frightened, and I was just as frightened as they were."

"After dark?"

"Yes, after midnight; in fact, it was early morning, just before daybreak. I was sound asleep and they woke me up and I heard their conversation."

"You heard them? Did they say anything about Magrigger?"

"Yes, I overheard the men use that name as the man whom one Rheinhardt had killed with an axe."

"Ah ha, there's where he killed Magrigger. Murder will out, and Rheinhardt's back will go up against a tree for this some day or I am not Captain Ike Livingstone."

"Boy, you're lucky to be alive I've never known Oscar Rheinhardt to be afraid of man or beast, and how he missed putting a bullet through you is beyond my ken."

After going into the cave a second time and examining the contents of the cave a little more closely, he again addressed his remarks to Hector.

"Say lad, I'm going to help myself in a bottle or two. Magrigger is dead, and these belong now to whoever finds them. A dead man cannot take his whiskey to Heaven with him."

A few bottles and a box of sea-biscuits were conveyed to the boat.

"Jump in, boy," he ordered, as soon as these were safely on board.

"What in blazes have you in that basket?" he asked with more than passing curiosity, Observed Hector preparing to bring it on the boat with him.

Hector looked up but did not answer.

"What have you there?" he again asked, but now somewhat impatiently.

"Oh, just the bones of a skeleton that I found buried near the cave."

"Bones? A skeleton bones? And what are you thinking of doing with them?" he asked sternly.

I thought of taking them with me. They'll be a help in my studies when I get back to college this Fall."

"You'll take no dead man's bones on this boat tonight. And more especially as seeing its the bones of Magrigger, and me with his wife and son on the craft."

The words came out with such decided emphasis, that Hector was convinced there would be no withdrawal from the decision on the part of the Captain. "No you can't take them. This schooner would never again reach shore if we took them on board."

"Shall I put them back in the cave, then?"

"Put them anywhere, but not here," he answered decisively. Hector carried them back carefully and reverently set them away in a corner of the cave. The story of a past tragedy was now being associated with the contents of his basket and were taking upon themselves a value in his mind second only to that of a living personality. In a sense he was relieved that his gruesome discovery was not going to be a companion of his on this uncertain journey now being undertaken.

As he took his seat in the dinghy, he hardly knew whether it were best of him to be going to La Cloche in company with fisher-folk and whiskey or whether a more favourable turn in his career would not have followed if he had stayed on the island until the Indians should return, for he was convinced that they meant to return, whatever their reason for not taking him with them that morning.

"Here Jack, come and take these," called out the Captain when they reached the side of the schooner.

The man addressed was Jack Conossoway, an Indian in age about middle life, who, with

His wife and son, comprised the crew of the vessel. In height and weight, he was considerably above the average. His black hair was cropped close around his head and ears, according to the reputed fashion with the Whig politicians in the time of the Stuarts. Though reputed to be an Ottawa, his face had the appearance of a Deleware while his size indicated a leaning towards the Neutrals, a tribe to which his grandmother traditionally belonged. His son, Louis, was a youth about seventeen years of age, and in appearance a typical Ottawa.

The Captain handed him the case of biscuits, remarking as he did so, "A lucky find, biscuits Magrigger," addressing his remarks to a white woman, who with her son, comprised the remaining occupants of the schooner.

"MacGregor," repeated Hector to himself, as he heard the Captain mention the name.

"Casting his eyes observantly towards her, he noticed a refined and gentle lady, a little past the meridian of life and quite apart in the appearance from what one might expect to meet in this regions, travelling on an ordinary fish-schooner. She was dressed in black, and had a pleasant countenance, yet one on which a look of compressed care was deeply imprinted. Beside her son, an interested spectator of Hector, as he approached in the dinghy with Captain Ike.

"We struck a cache on the island, and I helped myself to a couple of bottles and a box of biscuits," the Captain continued. "The biscuits will be for you Missus Magrigger, seeing as you don't indulge in this other." This remark was followed by an hilarious laugh, which served to show how well pleased he was with the discovery.

"You'll let me have one of the bottles for medicine though, will you not, Captain? I always like to have some around in case of sickness." Mrs. McGregor spoke in a pleasant manner and gentle tone of voice, but behind her request there was considerable anxious concern for she was fearful of the disastrous consequences which would likely follow over-indulgence of the liquor on the part of the Captain and his crew.

"Sure! Here it is," he answered as he handed one of the bottles to her.

"Let me have the other and I'll hold it up for you until you get up, Captain," she added, when she had secured possession of the one.

"All right, Missus Magrigger, but mind you don't drink them both."

"Not at all, Captain. I'll leave yours on the table in the cabin," she answered, and went forth to apparently do so.

As soon as he had disposed of the biscuits and bottles, he turned his attention to Hector "Here Louis, give the lad a hand," he instructed the Indian youth, in order that Hector might be assisted to make a landing in the deck of the vessel.

"Jump out boy," hay." he added, with a. mildness of tone, which betokened a spirit of sympathy awakened towards him.

Instead of the Indian, it was the white lad who jumped to his assistance. Reaching forth a hand, he said:

"Lean all your weight on it. I'll hold with this other.

Secure in his hold on the bowsprit behind, he enabled Hector to lift himself up easily over the side and reach the deck.

"I thank you," said Hector, appreciatively, as soon as he reached the deck.

From the first Hector found himself attracted to this youth whom he discerned would be about his own age. In height they were both about equals, but in size and weight Charlie MacGregor, for that was his name, had very much the disadvantage Lithe in his figure, quick in his movements, artistic in appearance, and of nervous temperament, he looked the part of the cultured youth he was in reality. Cheerful and pleasant to look upon, he carried little or no laughter on his face, the laughter being in his eyes else he cared to be merry.

"This is Charlie, my boy; Charlie MacGregor," his mother announced, when she came back, as she introduced him to Hector, in order that the two boys might find in one another congenial companionship.

"Hector MacLeod is my name," the rescued youth announced in response to this introduction, but for the benefit not only of Mrs. MacGregor, but of all who were now standing about him on the vessel, solicitous now how he chanced to be at such a place and all alone.

"Hector MacLeod!" repeated Mrs. MacGregor, with a surprised tone of voice. "Why that is the name of the man I have come up here to meet; an Indian trader and explorer who was partner with my husband."

"I had a grand-uncle by that name," Hector informed his new acquaintance, "whom my grandfather said was last seen at the La Cloche. They haven't heard of him for the last thirty years, though."

"Oh, dear!" Mrs. MacGregor heaved a sigh. "The last letter I had from Charlie's was six years ago," Following this parchment she drew from her breast a distorted and worn envelope, out of which extracted a letter, written neatly on thin birch-bark paper and handed it to Hector to read. In the dim light of the fast-waning twilight Hector was able to decipher its contents,—

DEAR FANNY,—

By the time you get this letter I will have started back to you and little Charlie. I have good news to tell you, almost too good to be true. Our cherished hopes are realized at last, and when I get back, you'll be able to lift your head equal to your station. So bye-bye until the ocean's no longer between us.

Lovingly,
CLAIRE

As Hector read the letter, Mrs. MacGregor continued: "Yes, six years and have been one long nightmare, which I possibly could not have endured but for the companionship of my boy. I was beginning to get over the rack of it when this letter came and she pulled out a second. This she handed to Hector also, as soon as he was through reading the first. It was written on the same kind of material as the other, but with a bolder though not as an artistic a hand.

> DEAR FANNY,—
>
> Word has come to me that you had been at the La Cloche looking for Claire. He left here six years ago, and we have reason to believe that he met with foul play. He had much mining property of great value which he sold, the money for which is here vet. If you get this, meet me at the La Cloche in October, but watch your steps and a trader by the name of Rheinhardt. Trusting we may have the good fortune to meet there at the time appointed.
>
> Faithfully yours,
HECTOR MACLEOD

When Hector read this letter and saw the signature of one who might be the very one of his own family whom his grandfather hoped he would locate, a spirit of buoyant hope began to loom up in his heart.

"It is October now, Mrs. MacGregor. That means that to-morrow you will be able to meet this trader."

"Tomorrow, if he is there, Hector; but it has always been to-morrow, and to-morrow, in the last six years, so that I have ceased to seek for anything now until it is in my hand.

I have Charlie, though, and I ought to be thankful that I am not left absolutely alone, and be more appreciative to God for his goodness in giving me him in place of my husband."

Hector still held the letter in his hand and was looking at it steadily. He saw a name and it was the one the Captain said had murdered MacGregor. He also remembered the observations of Reverend Monseigneur Marchand concerning the same man.

"He mentions a man here the name Rheinhardt." He spoke somewhat hesitatingly, not knowing the attitude of her mind toward him.

"Yes, I met him when I was at the La Cloche, a coarse, beastial German. It makes me shudder every time I think of him. They say"—and she spoke with timid fear as she repeated it—"that he is the one man most feared and hated on the lakes from fort William to the Penetang."

"I don't think I'd be afraid of him even although he did murder your husband," Hector repeated this statement slowly and there was no lack of courage in the spirit which inspired it.

"Murdered my husband!" she exclaimed, in a voice so loud that she was overheard by every one on the vessel. "Murdered! Who told you that?"

"I found three skeletons on the island, one at one place and two at another where I was last night. Besides, some trading men were there through the night and I overheard them say so." Hector repeated this in the same quiet and low tone of voice.

"Captain Ike, Captain Ike, come here!" she shouted, hysterically. "This boy says that my husband is over there on the island. Is that so, Captain Ike?"

The Captain, with a bottle in his hand containing the liquid in which his heart delighted, came over to where the three were standing.

"Is that so, Mrs. Magrigger?" He repeated her own words after her. "Well, bones is bones, and if they're not Magrigger's, they're somebody else's. That boy has found them. Were they Magrigger's or the French-son's, I don't know. They're there, all right and the boy says truth when he says they're there. If you want to know whose bones they are, ask Rheinhardt."

"Is Rheinhardt a murderer?" asked Mrs. MacGregor, askance, Must she add this also to his other achievements in crime and vice of which she had heard?

"Is Rheinhardt a murderer, Missus Magrigger? Rheinhardt would murder his own mother for the price of a bottle of whiskey, that's Reinhardt, if you ask me."

When he delivered himself to this judgment, "Here, Jack, come here," he called out.

Conossoway was craning his head forward listening to the conversation, with an animated expression on his face and a fire in his eye, which, if Rheinhardt could have seen, would have soon convinced him on which side, in respect to friendship, to slate the Indian. He came forward on the word of invitation from Captain Ike.

"We've got the rat in the hole at last Jack. Take a swig."

He handed him the bottle, which the Indian took eagerly and helped himself generously to a draught.

"Rusty Brown will soon have to hand off His money to you and me, Jack. Yes, we've got the rat in the hole at last, and it will be all day with him before he gets out again.

Hector was all attention at the mention of Rusty Brown's name.

"What has Rusty Brown got to do with it?" he enquired, as he observed this tragical drama of frontier life becoming increasingly complicated.

"Rusty Brown promised Jack and me and any Indian a handful of American Eagles, if we could find out one murder Rheinhardt committed and could prove it. We found lots of his murders, but not one which we could prove, and proof was what Rusty wanted, But now, we've got him."

"Here, Jack, have another, and then get back."

The invitation did not need repeating. The fast disappearing liquid was both the evidence of the uncontrolled taste of the two men and a cause of anxious concern respecting their future movements on the part of Mrs. MacGregor, though she had taken precautionary measures if possible to avert them.

CHAPTER XI

THE HAUNTED ISLAND LIGHTS

"Jack, you black Injun, come here," the Captain called out in a loud imperative.

The liquor was already having its expected results.

"Come here," he repeated more loudly when that individual did not put in an immediate appearance.

When the Indian approached, "Here, you take that," he said, as he handed out to him a bottle with a goodly portion of liquor still in it. "Give your old squaw some, and both of you get off to roost. Louis and I'll look after the craft until the morning."

Conossoway grinned audibly as the Captain proffered him the bottle. Reaching forth his hand he eagerly accepted it, gulped down a second generous helping, and then hurried off to his spouse as he was commanded. Following this, the Captain led Hector to the cabin where was prepared a meal for him. A simple repast comprising tea, bread and cold pork.

Sitting down at the table together, the Captain listened with intense interest as he related the experiences which had forced him to be separated from his companions and the camp. When he told of his sickness in the hut, and the timely appearance of the mascot, the Captain drank a sip to the dog's health. When he mentioned the episode of being thrown into a canoe by a drunken Indian, he another to the curse of the whole tribe, although, as Hector afterwards learned, one-quarter of his own blood belonged to that same race of people.

"Say, lad," he suggested, after Hector had finished with his supper, "if you want to have a back at the sights, you'd better get along to. You'll likely find him hanging on to the mainsail."

Hector readily availed himself of the opportunity, and going up on deck, found and Charlie both standing at the fore part of the vessel. The sails were all fully posted and fastened taut. The wind was blowing a steady, but not a severe breeze from the south by the south-west, and the vessel was moving along magnificently under its new management.

"Are there any rocks?" enquired Hector, as he seated himself on a package of goods being freighted for the fisherman at the Bustards.

"Lots of them to the right and shoals, too," was the answer of Louis, "but we take care to keep out of their way after night."

He spoke pure English, with no appreciable alien accent, giving abundant evidence that it was the tongue with which he was now most familiar.

The black waters alone lay in view immediately before them, dimly lighted by the weak rays of a new moon, shining down from an unclouded sky.

"Will the Captain take charge soon?" enquired Hector.

"He may, but I would be better pleased if he didn't," was the thought of Louis since he observed the extent of the captain's indulgence.

"Do you drink?" enquired Hector of Louis. He was apparently evincing a curiosity to find out to what extent the Indian race was being influenced by this pernicious evil.

"No, I never touch it. I'm a Christian."

"Good for you!" answered Hector, admiringly. "Is the Captain a good seaman?"

"Good, when he is sober, none better, but he never can quit when he gets a taste."

"The chances are not very good for tonight, then, for he was still going it strong when I came away."

"I think mother doctored their bottles," Charlie added, by way of creating a more hopeful outlook. "The half-breed doctor at Penetang gave her some, for he knew of the Captain's failing. 'A little medicine and a good long sleep after, is the only remedy,' he said. If she has, we'll have the ship to ourselves for the night."

Hardly had these words been spoken then the footsteps of the Captain were heard approaching. When he came up he took the helm from Louis and immediately turned the schooner facing westward. Both boys looked at each other, but neither made any remark. Then he had continued this course a little while, he ordered Louis back to the helm and commanded him to strike for the Indian village at the Cave of the Spirit, following which he lay down on the deck and was soon fast asleep.

"Is that place on the way to the La Cloche?" enquired Hector, for he was puzzled to know why the course of the vessel was altered.

"Oh, no. It is twenty-five miles out of our way, at least," answered Louis.

"Then why the change?" asked Hector.

"Going to see his friends, of course, and give them a clue as to the discovery made of the Island Cave. There'll be a procession to the cache as soon as they find out how much liquor has been lying there six years without an owner."

"Now for the La Cloche," spoke out Louis as he heard the deep snores of the Captain behind him.

The sails began to hang limp and Charlie and Hector went to investigate the cause. They found Jack Conossoway fast asleep. They shook him vigorously to awaken him but it availed nothing. There was not the slightest response to their continued effort. They called Mrs. MacGregor, for they deemed her counsel would be required if the two adult members of the crew were to spend the night in drunken unconsciousness.

"Now we have them where we want them," she exultingly asserted as she viewed his prostrate condition. "I doctored the bottle and one whiff was enough to set them quiet., but these two have taken enough for six. You have to give an overdose to have any effect on an Indian."

"Shall we not lift him up and set him on a berth?" suggested Hector.

"What's the use?" was her impatient answer. "He's too drunk to know the difference between the deck and a berth and, anyway, the deck is good enough for him."

It did not require any acute understanding to observe Mrs. MacGregor found congenial environment in neither her surroundings nor her companions.

"Do you know anything about these taut?" she asked Hector as she pointed to the sails.

"A little," was his answer. "I can keep the boat going if Louis can keep it straight."

"I am glad you know something about them," she said, as she saw him take hold and fix them taut in the face of the wind.

"Never fear, Mrs. MacGregor," he assured her as the sails began to hold their own, the wind now driving against them with increasing strength.

As the vessel cut the waters and moved rapidly forward under its new management, Mrs. MacGregor devoted her time in passing to and fro from the hold to the deck, assuring herself that nothing amiss was happening.

Everything was going along magnificently, when the shrill imperative of Charlie rang out.

"Look out, Louis," an island before you!" he saw a dark object immediately ahead.

"Island!" exclaimed Louis with surprise. Then it must be the Black Cloud.

"Looks like an island," remarked Hector slowly, as he kept scanning the waters in the direction of the object which appeared to the other two as an island. Hardly had he spoken, when three lights appeared on its surface.

The three stood silently and watched them come and go at intervals.

"Strange!" said Hector after a long silence and watching of the dancing lights. "You people certainly see strange things on the waters. I used to hear about them, but I never believed them true."

But while he yet spake, the three lights formed themselves into one, and mounted upward a luminous body towards the sky, not unlike the shape of a pear, but ten times its size, and moved gradually northwestward, increasing in rapidity the nearer it approached its destination, and then suddenly descended earthward, and went out of sight somewhere among the mountains of the La Cloche.

Still the boys made no remark. A feeling akin to fearsome awe possessed their spirits. After an interval they saw the dark object, which they had taken for an island, move and fly skyward, and continued mounting upward still best to view in the darkness and the height in which it reached.

"A cloud," interpreted Hector, who was the first to break the silence.

"I notice before I saw them there," reflected Louis in a subdued and reverent tone, ignoring the cloud and thinking only of the lights. "This is the third time, but I'll not see them again."

"Not see them again! Why? asked Hector in surprise.

"They are never seen more than three times by the same person."

Hector looked at Charlie, expecting to see a smile of credulity at the young Indian's explanation, but instead his face appeared under the dim light of the waning moon, sad and serious. His large, soft, gray eyes looked dreamily out on the waters before him, as if he were interpreting some message or unravelling the mysteries concerning the spirit world, the occult symbols of' which had in these visions of the night been placed before them.

"I must go and see mother," he informed them, and went quietly to her couch in the hold, where he expected to find her.

She was lying on it widely awake, turning over in her mind the story of Hector, and the probable murder of her husband, wondering if it were true, why it was not discussed before. She knew that Captain Ike was confident that it was he whom Hector had discovered, and was assured he was murdered. Was, then, her husband a whiskey trader? And did he achieve his success at the expense of the poor Indians? The thought was far from pleasant to her. As she was casting these things in her mind, Charlie stole quietly up and stood by her side.

"Mother, we have seen Devil's Island or something like it."

"Devil's Island! Did you see anything?"

"Yes, lights."

"How many?"

"Three."

"High or low?"

"Low."

"Did Hector see them?"

"Yes"

"Louis?"

"Yes. He said this was the third time, but would not again see them."

"Three times," she repeated to herself, in a low tone of voice. "I wish we were through on this trip. The thing I have been dreading by this past years has come at last. I do wish we were at the La Cloche, and I hope Hector MacLeod be there to meet us."

"But if the Captain had his way, we would not be going to La Cloche now, mother. He changed the course of the schooner and ordered Louis to take us to the Cave of the Spirit."

"Dear, dear. Fifty miles of a journey for nothing, and the Lord alone knows what might happen before it was ended."

Just then the schooner took a lurch and swung unexpectedly to the right. Something had happened.

Mrs. MacGregor came up and joined the boys, who stood watching for a considerable period after the apparition had disappeared. Hearing the heavy breathing of the prostrate Captain, she went over and spoke in a low tone of voice, "I do wish he would wake up. They took enough for six," she commented under her breath. "I hope it is not one of them."

She was evidently expecting a death to follow the appearance of the lights and she began to be afraid lest she unwittingly had done a harm where she intended only to safeguard the boys, herself and the vessel.

Louis went back and took hold of the helm with a firm hand and Hector, always alert and active by nature, began to bestir himself for the safety of their movements.

"Is Louis cool?" he enquired of Charlie when the two boys stood apart by themselves some little time later.

"Oh, I think so. He is very observant and has made this trip more than a dozen times in full charge. He knows all the islands, the shoals, and the shelters. I think we are quite safe under his care."

While they were speaking the vessel gave a second lurch to the right.

"What is it? Has anything happened?" exclaimed Mrs. MacGregor out of breath as she ran to Louis.

"It is that dark object again come back, Mrs. MacGregor, and the water is getting shallower. It is there like an island lying out straight before us."

Mrs. MacGregor peered through the darkness but observed nothing save a little space of water lighted up by the dim rays of the waning moon. A soft Wind fanned her face as she looked westward.

"I see nothing, Louis, but the wind is rising and if it does, that means an impossible passage to the La Cloche to-night."

By this time both of the other boys had joined Mrs. MacGregor and Louis.

"An optical illusion, I am afraid, Louis," Hector suggested after several instants of silent gazing. "It may have been only a cloud."

"That may be," answered Louis, "but whatever it was, I saw it plainly. The lights and shadows on the bay oftentimes deceive us after night."

"A cloud and an island can hardly be distinguished in the day, if the spectre of both happens to be lying on the horizon," continued Hector in an effort to explain the phenomenon.

"That is certainly true," added Mrs. MacGregor, "especially in the early morning I can remember Captain Ike himself on one occasion vowing a cloud, which he saw, to be a distant island, and we all thought the same thing until we came close enough and then found it to be a cloud."

"Can we be near land?" Hector asked, detecting a sound which appeared to him like a waterfall. His hearing was apparently more acute than that of the others, for they, as yet, had heard nothing. "It may be the mainland we are seeing."

"Why, yes, we may be," answered Louis. "The mainland is over there and we must be quite close to it."

To the mind of Mrs. MacGregor, the discovery of a body of land in their immediate neighbourhood was a fortunate circumstance. She was not too much enamored with the journey across the bay after night.

If it's a river there'll be a landing at its mouth, and if so we had better pull in there for the night. It will give us time to get a few hours of rest at any rate," she said, making the desire of her mind to call a halt to the further travel until the reappearance of daylight. In this conclusion she was convinced by the incident of having two drunken person lying prostrate on the deck, one fore and the other aft, and the uncertainty of their conduct might be when they would both awaken.

Louis hesitated. "The shore is very irregular here, Mrs. MacGregor, and there is no telling the moment you may strike a submerged rock, a small island or a sand bank, and it's a dark night."

Louis well knew the dangers to navigation on the bay when too proximate to its shore line. Had they a certain knowledge of their whereabouts, decision would have been easy, but the night and the various incidents connected with it had filled his mind with misgiving awe, as he looked upon these varied phenomena, the premonitions of some impending fate.

"There is nothing like trying," suggested Hector. "We can make frequent use of a sounding line and avoid danger in that way."

The counsel of Mrs. MacGregor prevailed. The vessel was turned landward and made to move cautiously, as they sought to obtain entrance to the mouth of the river. Once there were in great danger as they passed over a submerged rock, but by continuous and frequent use of the sounding line it was detected and avoided. Soon they reached the current made by the outflowing waters of the river.

"We are there now, Louis," Charlie exclaimed as he discovered the moving waters with the channel deepening.

They kept on sailing until they got far enough inland to escape the swelling of the bay and its storms, should any arise, and then drew in near the shore.

"Throw out the anchor, Hector," Louis requested. "We'll snag her up tight at the stern in addition, and lay to until we get ready to move out in the morning."

Hector picked up the mass of iron and threw it overboard with the same ease with which Louis was accustomed to see Captain Ike handle it.

"My, you must be strong," remarked Charlie, as he saw it tossed into the air. "I wish I had your muscle."

"When it had floated down the full length of his anchor chain they fastened the other end with the aid of the dinghy to a large oak bark and were back on their vessel awaiting impatient, for the night when Hector recalled, "Charlie, I hear a paddle."

The moon had now disappeared and the night was quite dark. Dip, dip, dip, gently and at long intervals they heard it. A canoe was drawing away from the schooner. Of this there could be no doubt.

"Some Indian disturbed in his sleep and come over to see who we are," was Charlie's explanation.

When the sound of the canoe moved away out of hearing, Charlie and Hector retired together, and were discussing the event of the day in the interval before going to sleep especially the appearance of the phantom island.

"I thought I heard that canoe again but I must be mistaken," Hector observed, when in a lull of their conversation he recognized the movements immediately near them of a loitering canoe.

Both boys got up, and leaning over the side of the vessel peered out into the night but nothing could be observed in the near vicinity. They returned to their resting places and resumed their light hearted talk for their minds were not in the least affected by so little an incident as the passing of a tramp canoe.

Soon Charlie was asleep, but Hector lay awake like ruminating on the strange vicissitudes that were now pouring into his life from every unexpected quarter. He thought of the guardians of the vessel paralyzed in drunkness, the bereft woman with a slender boy her alone protector, the object of their visit in the La Cloche, the name of the trader whom she was going to meet, when a third time he heard the dip of the paddle in the water. Because of the complete stillness that reigned, he heard it distinctly and there was no mistaking that a canoe was loitering about for some reason or other. Hector lay quiet, listening to it passing around the schooner until at last he heard it pull away. It was the more distinctly heard the further it got, the paddler apparently less precautious of the probability of being overheard lessened. Hector rose up and looked out in the direction on which he heard it depart, but saw nothing in the darkness which seemed to grow blacker and blacker the longer he looked out on it. Discerning nothing, he returned to his couch and was soon asleep, totally oblivious to the stirring events which awaited only the appearance of daylight to force themselves upon them.

CHAPTER XII

UNDER THE SHADOW OF THE WHISKEY TRADER'S LODGE

The gray dawn was just beginning to loom up on the eastern horizon when Hector found himself wakened up by Charlie.

"Jump up quickly," he requested in a sharp excited voice.

Hector was up on his feet instantly.

"What's up? Anything wrong?" he eagerly enquired.

That man Rheinhardt is sitting down on the bank a little below us with a rifle in his hand, and Mother thinks we'd better get ready and sail out."

"Is he alone?"

"He is just now."

"Where's your Mother?"

"Didn't she sleep at all last night?"

I don't suppose. I think from what she says that a canoe was prowling around all night."

"I suppose there's nothing to fear from that fellow?"

"Nothing, if he lets us get away quietly; but we're in for a rough time if he finds out we have whiskey and money on board and the Captain and Conossoway dead drunk."

"Whiskey and money?"

"Yes, a barrel of rum, and a cask of brandy and the fishermen's pay for the season.

"Is Rheinhardt a thief?"

"Don't know. The Captain and Conossoway think he is."

"Where is the Captain now?"

"Still asleep."

Hector looked over in his direction, saw his sleeping form in the very position where he lay the night before, and heard him breathe with the same regularity.

"How long will that last?" he asked.

"I don't know, Mother says that they are due to wake up any time now, but a drunk Indian is better asleep than awake any time.

By the time the two boys were afraid. The trader had left the shore and gone into the woods.

When Mrs. MacGregor appeared, "Now is the time for us to get away," she counselled urgently. "His men are hidden somewhere near, I am sure, and they'll be watching every move we make. Charlie, go down and untie the line and we'll get out right away. I wonder where are we anyway?"

"I'll untie the line," volunteered Hector.

"I think you had better not show yourself, since his men saw you in the cave, and if they knew you they would turn their rifles on you in a moment."

That was a view-point of the situation which had not occurred to Hector. His presence was creating an awkward situation for the rest of them.

"I wish I had different clothes on," he remarked.

"What about putting on the Captain's coat?" suggested Charlie. "They'll certainly not know you in his clothes."

Hector reached out his hand and took it from the nail in the mast on which it hang.

"That's a good idea, Charlie. I'll try it on anyway."

Hector was muscular, and in size not far inferior to Captain Ike himself.

"It's not to great a misfit, after all," he said, as he buttoned it on. "This will do we well. Now for a handkerchief around my head and the disguise will be complete."

Charlie laughed out as he saw the transformed appearance. Both of the boys were in the best of good humour, for neither of them anticipated any interference with their movements by any persons on the shore.

"Aha, here's something we may need," Hector exclaimed, more by way of jest than of serious import, as his eyes rested on the Captain's rifle, standing up in a corner where he still lay in restful sleep. "It's a beauty," he added as he examined it with pleasure.

Hector was the chief of marksman of the camp. Notwithstanding miscarriage which befell him in respect to the partridge he seldom missed the bull's-eye in a fifty year test, and he could be counted on giving a good account of himself in anything within three hundred yards.

"I wonder if there is any ammunition about?" he enquired.

"It's loaded, Hector. The Captain always carried it ready for he said that an empty gun is of no use to any one."

"Yes, it's loaded." Hector assented, "but I should like some ammunition in case . . ." he did not finish the sentence.

Charlie pointed to the powder-horn and the shot-bag hung above the rifle. "There they are, Hector."

Hector reached and took them down and fastened them on his body as if prepared to go out on a hunting trip. The boys again looked down the bank and this time saw Rheinhardt pondering along with his rifle over his shoulder.

In the meantime, Mrs. MacGregor had awakened Louis who was also in readiness to get the schooner unloosed from its moorings in obedience to her wish. Charlie had started to the shore to untie the rope that fastened the stern of the vessel to the moorings, while Louis and Hector, at the capstan, began drawing in the anchor. When Rheinhardt saw these preparations being made to move out he hastened his steps and arrived just as Charlie had the line in his hand and was prepared to get back on the dinghy.

There is an old saying that whom the wish the gods wish to destroy they first make mad. Perhaps it was this which made Rheinhardt act so foolishly on that early October morning towards the son of the man whose blood cried out from the rocks of Cave Island for justice. Perhaps, and this is the more likely reason, that the acts of self-destruction, which characterized the life of Rheinhardt, had now come to their culminating point and the end to which all these years he had been moving had now arrived.

Louis had moved over to the side near the shore and was nearest to Rheinhardt of those on the vessel when he arrived,

"Hello there, Louis, is Captain Ike around?" he inquired of him, recognizing the identity of the schooner.

Mrs. MacGregor, fearing that Louis might inform Rheinhardt that the Captain was still in drunken sleep came over by his side. He immediately recognized her.

"Hello, Missus Magrigger; you're having fine weather for your trip. Where's Captain Ike?"

"He's in bed, of course, were all honest folks ought to be at this time of day."

"Aha," he answered with a chuckle, " and I suppose that's the reason you and I are about."

" We're here to wait for the daylight," she answered in a quiet tone of voice, "but what are you here for?"

"Oh, just to see what a tramp boat is doing sneaking around these waters in the middle of the night."

Charlie was now standing with the rope in his hand.

"Charlie," she said to her son, "you had better get on board, and let us be off."

"You're not going away until I see Captain Ike, Missus Magrigger," and with that he reached out to his right hand and took a strong hold of Charlie by the collar of his coat.

"Let that boy go," she shouted at him.

To answer to Mrs. MacGregor's peremptory command, he looked down at the slender boy by his side with a grin which meant the utter futility of resistance to his will. A few moments' silence followed her request for the release of Charlie. Rheinhardt was a man who was not to be hurried into doing anything which was not in accord with his own wishes. Should one get a square look into his shifty blue eyes, which was a feat seldom accomplished, he would see there a feature bespoke cruelty as well as cunning. The inability to get any response from Captain Ike, and the unsatisfactory answer Mrs. MacGregor, convinced Rheinhardt's already disturbed mind that there was a sinister motive accounting for the presence of the schooner in these unfrequented waters. He therefore determined to hold the vessel until a rigorous examination were made of all the circumstances accounting for its presence there.

Mrs. MacGregor was filled with fear and anger when she saw her boy held in the clutches of a character who would go for the lengths, no matter how unreasonable to accomplish his own ends.

"Will you not let that boy go?" she therefore repeated with increased anger.

Up to this time Hector had kept himself out of view, but curious to see, as well as to hear what was going on, he came out from behind the freightage and saw for the first time the man who was reputed to be the one most feared and followed of any on the bay. There he stood,, six feet in height, powerfully built, a true picture of a well-trained over-developed German soldier. His bullet-shaped head was set on a short thick neck. His face was round and bloated, showing an excessive use of intoxicants. Looking at Mrs. MacGregor, his mouth opened with an attempt at a smile and showed teeth of size and shape which betokened his fitness for a carnivorous beast. The butt of his rifle, which he now hold in his left and, rested on the ground.

"He'd be an ugly man to meet in a scrap," thought Hector, as he saw his continued disregard of Mrs. MacGregor's wishes, and deterred if resistance were continued, to the eventuality it might lead.

"Will you call the Captain, Missus Magrigger?"

Rheinhardt spoke in a conciliatory tone as if to assure her that he only stood on the most friendly of terms with her.

At this juncture Charlie made an effort to release himself from the hold of Rheinhardt, but this only served to make him grip him with more determined obstinacy. In order In convince the boy that there was to be no disregard to his will, he twisted the collar of his coat, tightening it with a strangle hold upon his neck. The blood rushed to Charlie's face and he gasped with signs of extreme discomfort.

Hector had been taught that the first step towards a successful issue in a combat was to disarm the antagonist, but how could a helpless boy accomplish such a feat in the hands of so powerful an enemy? Hector knew that the power denied to Charlie was within near reach of himself.

"You beast, you, let that boy go," she exclaimed with anger.

Rheinhardt had all the stubbornness of a tyrant as well as the unfeeling cruelty of a criminal. The language of the source couched in so imperative a command. The only one effect and that the worst possible on a nature which had already attained to the superlative degree in stubbornness. He gripped hold of Charlie's collar with increased discomfort to the boy.

On Hector MacLeod, quick witted and resourceful, fearless and gallant, the request of Charlie's mother had an opposite effect. It called his energy, both of mind and body, into quick and fruitful action. Seeing that Rheinhardt was giving no evidence of releasing Charlie, he took up the Captain's rifle and brought it into line ready for an emergency. Hardly had the words of Mrs. McGregor reached the ears of Rheinhardt when his side was shot out of his hand and its stock shattered, and he heard a whizz of the bullet of his own disabled rifle discharged as it went off by the catastrophe which befell it.

At the place where Hector rested on one edge, secluded from view of Rheinhardt, a small cloud of smoke curled up from the end of Captain Ike's rifle, which was quickly loaded for further emergency. Captain Ike himself turned over on his couch at the report so near his body, but gave no further evidence of waking up.

So sudden, unexpected and disastrous was this intervention that in his unnerved surprise Rheinhardt dropped his hold upon Charlie, and did not regain his self-possession before the boy had leaped into the dinghy and climbing up was soon standing on deck by the side of his mother.

The boat released was now directed into mid-stream by Louis and began moving down slowly with the current.

Rheinhardt pulled out his whistle, gave a loud shrill call ordering his men into action Himself hastened back into the woods and soon reappeared a little further down the shore with a fresh rifle and two of his men carrying a canoe.

In the meantime Louis had taken the helm and was steering the vessel into mid-channel and out for the open waters.

Rheinhardt's canoe shot out from the shore to head the schooner off. He placed himself at the head and shouted with a stentorian voice to Louis to direct the vessel to the shore. As Louis refused he drew out His rifle in line with the Indian youth and his finger was just discovering the trigger when once again his rifle was shot of his hand. Foaming with rage he shouted he would get even with his invisible marksman, and again sounded his whistle over the waters, calling all his men to the combat.

By chance Hector observed a man lying in ambush near the shore and he, too, with his rifle in line with Louis at the helm.

"I'll wing that fellow," thought Hector aloud, and took immediate aim on this would be assassin.

When his rifle barked this third time, the bullet passed through the hand which held the rifle now drawn in deadly aim on Louis. The wounded man gave a shout as his rifle dropped from his partially paralyzed hand, acquainting the occupants of the canoe with the disaster which once more befell them.

"Did you hit him?" asked Louis, in great excitement.

"That I did, in the hand though."

"That means blood," the Young Indian stated.

"Better his than yours, Louis. 'Self Preservation is the first law of nature.' We have the schooner to save."

Hector was now aware that as blood was drawn, the fight must be to a finish. He knew enough of the self-appointed laws and custom of the region to expect no quarter. But he was master of himself, if not of the situation. He moved about without the least excitement, and thought and acted rapidly. Profiting by his own experience in a canoe, and seeing theirs was a birch-bark, he determined to sink it, and give the occupants a swimming chance for their lives. Loading with buck shot he took aim for the centre of the canoe at the water-line, and tore a hole on the side which admitted the water. The inflow soon began to fill the canoe to the imminent danger of all three in it, and Hector rewarded by seeing all its occupants swimming for the shore and safety.

"Thank God, Louis, we're safe."

But hardly were the words spoken when a woman's scream was heard. The two had jumped forward and beheld Mrs. MacGregor handed over the side of the schooner on a waiting canoe on the opposite side of the Schooner by two men who had boarded the vessel unnoticed.

"They've got us, Hector! Oh, poor Mother!" exclaimed Charlie, his voice quivering with emotion.

Not yet," answered Hector, with unwavering resolution, every muscle of his body

now tense for heated activity.

CHAPTER XIII

THE UNFORGOTTEN PAST LEAPS INTO THE LIMELIGHT

As soon as Charlie boarded the schooner, and Mrs. MacGregor saw the determination of Rheinhardt to again come in close quarters, she ordered Charlie to awaken Captain Ike, while she went to perform a similar service for Conossoway. She was energetically shaking him and succeeded in getting him in a sitting posture when she was seized by the two intruders who had obtained easy access to the deck, climbing up at the side at the stern.

While Charlie and Hector deck attention directed to that side of the river from which the leader, Rheinhardt, had made his attack, they were unaware that another contingent of men had been called from the farther side of the river unnoticed, they boarded the schooner, seized Mrs. MacGregor, dropped her into a waiting canoe and Carried her off helpless. Her screams were the first announcement to the boys of their successful arrival on the deck.

In order to better equip himself for action, Hector began hastily to unbutton the Captain's smock, which he wore.

"Off goes this disguise," he said, as he divested himself of it. "Whatever the consequences, I'll be in my true colours anyway,"

It was well he did so for Charlie had succeeded by this time in awakening the Captain out of his drunken stupor.

It was just then that the cry from Mrs. MacGregor came forth as if from the waters on the side of the vessel, "Charlie! Oh help—Char—," followed by a short scream, ending to a muffled sound as of a woman being pissed.

Leaping to his feet, the Captain cried out, "What's going on here, anyway?"

Seeing Hector with his rifle in his hand, and forgetting the incident of the night before, he rushed to the conclusion that this stranger was the cause of all tis turmoil. He leaped forward to seize him, but Louis by his equally quick movement threw himself between them, protesting vehemently, "No, No! This is the boy we took off the island last night. It is Rheinhardt's men at the stern. They're after the fisherman's money."

"Rheinhardt's men? And where are we anyway?"

"Tied up at the mouth of the Espanola," answered Louis. "We came here through the night when you were asleep."

"Me, asleep?"

In a trice the links of the chain of events of the night before stood out clearly before the Captain, as if no sleep had in the meantime intervened—the rescue of Hector, the discovery of the cache, the presence of the fisherman's money, while at the same time the commotion at the stern behind the freight age was becoming more distinct, the scuffling, shouting noises indicating that a conflict above the ordinary was going on.

"Rheinhardt's men after the money, aha!" he exclaimed, now fully awake to the situation.

Rushing to the scene they found the now awakened Jack Conossoway in mortal combat with two of the trader's men who were striving to overcome and pinion him, but Conossoway with an agility far above the average, was matching his one strength against their two with gratifying effect. Having got one by the font he had just succeeded in getting him down when the other, observing his comrade's danger, seized the capstan handle and swinging it over his shoulder was about to bring it down on the head of Conossoway when the Captain appeared on the scene.

Divining his intentions, the Captain leaped, but not too soon. Grasping the assassin's weapon he wrested it out of his-hand.

"It's you, Cadotte," he said, recognizing his assailant. "I'll teach you to be mixing yourself up in such dirty work."

Seizing him by the collar of his coat with one hand, held him off at arm's length while with the other he began to belabour him to the face, slapping with open palm, first the one cheek, then the other, with grim drunken on sight, while Cadotte, because of the greater strength of the Captain's arms, could do nothing to defend himself. After having satisfied himself that he had mauled him sufficiently, he pushed him to the railing and then pitched him headlong over into the water.

All this while Conossoway continued his strangle-hold on the man with whom he fought, until he lay an unconscious heap his feet. So motionless was he that Hector deemed him dead.

"Is he dead? He asked Conossoway.

"Dead! Who's dead?" snorted the Captain.

Seizing, lifting up, and shaking him. "Get up I tell you," he ordered the unconscious heap. But there was no response.

"Here, Jack, give us a lift."

Both took hold and swung him over the side to follow his mate into the water.

"Where is Mrs. MacGregor?" enquired of Hector.

Conossoway, taking poise of the manner of the Indian is on the alert, and stepping to the railing to make observation with both his eyes and ears, "Gone in canoe, me think," he said, as he pointed to the shore, the opposite to that to which they had tied up their hull the night before.

In the meantime, Louis had taken charge of the schooner and was steering the helm towards the open waters, while the traders on the shore discussed with one another the circumstances connected with the melee.

Rheinhardt was a good swimmer, as were all of his followers. There was little danger of their getting drowned so near the shore as they were when forced to abandon their canoe by Hector's clever marksmanship. It only a matter of a few minutes until he had hi men rallied again about him.

Where are the other two?" Rheinhardt asked, when he saw this number missing.

"They're across on the other shore at your own camp; they got the woman and handed her over to the Indians," answered one of his men.

The two men, who had been pitched so unceremoniously off the schooner into the water, were rescued easily by a comrade who was paddling over to take part in the conflict. The first of the two was able to assist in his own rescue, though, before he reached the shore his face had become so blackened by the aft repeated strokes of Captain Ike as to make him almost unrecognizable, and his face as swollen as to almost preclude the blood from reaching his eyes. The second was Fished out with more difficulty, but finally he also was dragged into the canoe, though in a state of semi-consciousness. Both were sitting on the shore when Rheinhardt and his men got back to their own side of the river.

"Who did you find on the schooner?" the trader quarried, addressing the man with the swollen face.

"Only them's that's always there," was the answer, not too courteous.

"Did you see Captain Ike?" Rheinhardt was anxious to obtain a knowledge of the strength of the crew and the personnel of the ones who had taken part I the fight.

"Well, I might say I did," answered Cadotte.

"I don't think ye'd see him now," interjected Hank Bryant as he looked scrutiningly into the battered man's face.

Hank Bryant was the jester of the wrests and more than one suffered discomfort at times from the readiness of his wit. He was not an employee of Rheinhardt, but of the North West Fur Company, of which that MacKenzie was the agent at the La Cloche.

Cadotte reported in spirit and by way of excuse for his condition, "But there was two I could have handled either one of them alone, but the two was too much for me."

"Ye needn't complain, fur ye've more of a face on ye now than ye had afore at any rate," commented the same Hank Bryant.

The laughter created by this retort was heartily joined in by all of the men, even Rheinhardt himself not refraining from showing his teeth by way of a smile.

"But who did the shooting? Didn't you see anything of the one who did the shooting?" The one anxiety now of the humiliated Rheinhardt was the discovery of the person or persons responsible for their defeat.

"It must have been Conossoway," suggested the one who had received the strangling by his hand, but who was now sufficiently to take part in the discussion. Notwithstanding the surmise of Hector that he had passed beyond the possibility of discovery, thanks to his douche in the water, hurt was the loss of a few ounces of liquid, followed afterwards by several days of comparative weakness.

"It wasn't Conossoway," protested Cadotte. "I tell you I was lying on the floor asleep when we got on board. We just got the woman when he sat up, rubbed his eyes, and then jumped and at us like a tiger. He got Jeff down, and was choking him, as you see he did, and I was just getting ready to put the finishing touch to the cur when Captain Ike jumped on my back, and when he got overpowered they both threw us out into the water, then ran off, the sneaking cowards, they did."

boy with his sleeves rolled up and a

"And was Captain Ike asleep too?" enquire Rheinhardt. "He didn't answer me, I know, but who then did the shooting if he was asleep? Were there other men beside Conossoway and Captain Ike on board?"

"Not that we saw," both answered together.

"It must have been that other boy," one repeated hesitatingly, as if trying to recall the detailed occurrences of the morning of events.

"A boy!" cried a chorus of them incredulously.

"Yes, a boy," he repeated with emptiness.

"a boy with his sleeves rolled up and a handkerchief tied round his neck, a quick-moving boy his with curly hair."

"And yer could see him? Ah, yes, but that was afore ye got yer present eyes," commented Bryant.

"He was a poor shot, whoever he was," added another.

"Poor shot! Nonsense!" protested the companion of Hank Bryant. "He didn't shoot to kill, anyone could see that. It was Rheinhardt's rifle he wanted to put out of commission and not Rheinhardt himself, and it's the same with the canoe. He could have killed the three of you with the same shots that sent down the canoe. Whoever he was, he didn't shoot to kill."

"But he hit one of our men," answered Rheinhardt.

"The blessings of the Virgin on him, if he did," soliloquized Bryant, in a low tone of voice but sufficiently loud to be overheard by Rheinhardt.

"He drew blood," re-asserted that trader in an angry voice.

Waiting with a thirst of revenge, he ordered his men to get ready for a renewal attack.

"We've got the woman," he gloated, "and that'll give us another chance to get at the them. They'll not leave without her," he assured himself.

Immediately everything was got in readiness for the second fight which all of them were confident would be soon impending.

Taking advantage of the occasion presented by these preparations, Bryant hurried back to his master, Rory MacKenzie, at his place of rendezvous up the river. In his unusual Irish brogue, he informed him of the capture, under instructions from Rheinhardt, of Mrs. MacGregor by a quartette of Indians expected that MacKenzie would start out immediately with his men, and range himself on the side of Captain Ike and the crew of the schooner.

Contrary to his expectations, MacKenzie listened to his tale with an air of complete indifference. To a stranger it might appear that he was not in the least concerned of the outcome of the conflict or the fate of Mrs. MacGregor. As a matter of fact, he had found Himself an unobserved spectator of the event, as he had also been his partner, MacLeod, and both of them, therefore, had first-hand knowledge of all which had transpired.

Bryant, when he had finished his story, could not hide his disappointment at this apparent indifference of MacKenzie.

"Are ye gone clean daft," he asked him, "to allow that man Rheinhardt to run the bay?"

"The schooner is not ours, Hank. Why then should we get mixed up with other people's quarrels?" was the answer given him. "If the schooner's crew drew blood, you know what that means. The man who is going to get ahead of Rheinhardt in the shedding of blood is not anywhere to be found between me and the Hudson.

"Now ye're wrong there, M'Kinzie. He's a good winner, a poor loser is Rheinhardt, and now he's beaten. I knowed to were goin' to be when he sterted. He's not doin' the wrong thing ivery day fur a month, and now he's doin' the durty wurrk in dealin' wimmen. I don't mind his sellin' to whiskey to them that want it, and hev the money to pay fur it, and I don't mind makin' it fur him, but there's no wumman-stealin' fur me. I'm dune with Rheinhardt that's what I say."

MacKenzie listened with apparent internal but made no remark.

"The wheel's turned, M'Kinzie," his servant continued. "The Fates have been his friend up till this, but as I telt ye, they're dune with him now. I can see it in every step. Them lights hevn't been hangin' around the bay fur nuthin'."

The light seen by the three occupants of the schooner the preceding night seen also by MacKenzie's men, and the imagination of Bryant had pictured thee as three spirits and that of those whom Rheinhardt had reputed MacKenzie to have done to death.

"The ghost of M'Grigger and the other one, I've seen them both in a fortnight, I see the lights sez there's another comin'. M'Grigger get murthered and the Injuns all tell that M'Kinzie's the murtherer!"

Hank Bryant repeated this last sentence slowly and with a subdued tone of voice, as if speaking to himself aloud rather than addressing MacKenzie.

The mention of his name in connection with two murders, MacKenzie resented with hot rage.

"What do you mean, Bryant?" he shouted, as he leaped to his feet. "Do you mean to tell me that this Rheinhardt, this Hessian officer, says that I'm a murderer?"

"It's yer own secret, as far as I'm concerned. The day'll niver come when I'll squeal on a M'Kinzie. Ye've lived a dacent life, and ye've acted the honest man, and except for the braining of M'Grigger, which was the fault of yer timper, and shooting of Flora MacLean, which may be called an accident, if so be ye did it, no man can raise a hand against either of us. We handled good stuff and gave every man good value fur his money, and if them Rheinhardt's men had let it alone, and let the dacent people make a decent livin'. Instead of wantin' to git it fur theirselves,

117

we could go on to the end and claim a dacent burial. But why ye allow that Rheinhardt to run the bay is more'n I can tell. Ye need to have some sinse, even with yer divil of a timper, but now yer losin' yer sinse and are keepin' on with yer timper till ye'll git Rheinhardt's bullet inter yer own brain instead of yours into Rheinhardt."

"Who says that I killed MacGregor?' MacKenzie interrupted, evincing the same passionate rage.

"Them that sez they knows, but don't yell so loud, seein' that they're not all yer friends who git yer money for their wurrk. Them's three spies ye've had here for the last three months, and they've helped to kidnap that wumman, but more'n one sez ye've brained MaGrigger, and it's his name that was on the claim with yersilf, and though it's not myself that's sayin' that's the raison, there's them that is sayin' it."

In the face of all this accusations MacKenzie sat staring into vacancy. Making no comment, Bryant continued:

"When ye git up against Conossoway, ye're gittin' up against them that are Injuns and Captain Ike, though he calls himself while has both their blud and their cunnin's and once they stert, they'll niver let up till one their bullet inter the brain of their inimy and they're sterted."

At this MacKenzie rose up and paced back and forth across the lodge, showing every evidence of being greatly perturbed. One looking on could easily discern that this was no ordinary man who thus kept his lodge hidden in the woods on this secluded shore of the bay. That martial tread was obtained only after years of military training. He looked the soldier in every movement and poise of his body but the soldier life makes the human mind put a cheap value on human life. If nations wipe out hundreds of thousands of lives to carry out their own will in the face of opposition of other nations, how can it be wrong for individuals to do the same thing? Does an act lose its criminality, the greater and more far-reaching it becomes? It reasoned Rheinhardt, and probably, too, MacKenzie, as they plied their trade and removed the obstacles out of the way to the accomplishment of their supremest ambitions.

The appearance of these lights on three consecutive nights, notwithstanding MacKenzie shouting the idea that they could have any significance for him, such as appealed to the superstitious mind of

Bryant, unconsciously were having their influence. Turning abruptly upon Bryant as he passed he threw the words into his face:

"Who did you hear saying that I killed MacGregor?"

"Them three fellows ye hev as spies. They sez, ye killed M'Grigger for the claim, for the names of both ye are on it."

"What do they know about the claim?"

"They know enuff to try and git it, and if Rheinhardt marries the wumman and gits the bairn out of the way, then there's but no other, and that's M'Kinzie. Rory M'Kinzie ye're playin' inter their hand, and yer can't see it. That divil of an Injun drew his rifle to kill the boy for Rheinhardt, but nayther of yez got yer way fur the hivens is against ye."

Again MacKenzie began to pace up and down his comfortable lodge, it, too, in no construction and furnishings, bearing evidence of the military mind that conceived it. Bryant ceased making further remarks and sat pondering the future, as MacKenzie saw apparently the past. Then, as if speaking aloud his own thoughts rather than addressing his servant:

"You think, Bryant, that these men are spies of Rheinhardt?"

"I know they be, M'Kinzie for I heerdt them with mine own ears. Would ye think that I'd lie to ye? If this wumman-stealin's goin' to be allowed, I'm dune, that's what I say."

In answer MacKenzie spoke cooly and collectedly as a man who had thought out satisfactorily his conclusions, "I don't accuse you of trying to deceive me, Bryant for I've been thinking myself for sometime that what you say about them may be true. If it is, and Rheinhardt does any harm to Fanny MacGregor, then his carcase shall never again walk alive on the shores of this river. There's a greater reason in my mind than the ownership of the claim, why that woman should be saved,"

"I knowed that, fur she's got the papers, as Captain Ike has, which he's lookin' after for her."

"Papers! What papers?"

"The papers that tells about the luvely girl ye killed, Flora MacLean."

At this MacKenzie took a leap into middle of the room, his face lighted up with a jealous passion, nursed and nourished in his breast these more than a score of years, while beads of perspiration began to come thickly out on his forehead.

"Who says that I shot Flora MacLean? Is it Rheinhardt?"

The paper sez that it's your gun which was found in the room, and if it's yer gun, then it's you that did the shootin'."

These papers were now in the possession of Bryant, which he had kept guardedly there for many years. Pulling the packet out of his pocket, he handed it to MacKenzie. They told of a young woman, the wife of a British officer, shot by another officer, the disappearance of the military murderer,, and the accusation that he had fled to Canada to escape his punishment.

For the first time, MacKenzie read the account of what was reputed his crime and escape, as told by the press of the west country, and the comments of that press on the crime.

Slowly he read the story of his desertion from the army, the finding of the pistol in the dead girl's room, and the conclusion based on two suspicious circumstances that it was he who had murdered her. He was known to have visited her frequently when his unit was stationed at the Beeches.

Putting down the paper, MacKenzie sat with his eyes dilated and staring into vacancy as of a man demented. Bryant, judging that the truth had reached its goal, added this further explanation, "It's yer timper, M'Kenzie, it's yer timper that's got ye inter all yer troubles."

But these words of the unabashed and faithful slave fell on deaf ears. MacKenzie still stared into vacancy, and so long that Bryant was beginning to fear that the reality of dementia had come with the appearance. Then suddenly, the man of action once more asserted himself.. Leaping up, and the fierce sight of rage again in his eyes, rage not against his minions an Rheinhardt and his crew, but rage against life itself—life which had slanderously made a criminal of him—life which had emptied his days of all worthy content—that was the life against which he now directed all his wrath.

"Bryant," he said, "Bryant, get up and bring that woman back safe from the hands of these men. If what you say about them is true, then

God forgive you if you don't bring back the woman unhurt or their carcases. Now, off with you; make sure work, m Ill" the attempt."

"New ye're spakin sinse; but it's their carcases ye'll get, M'Kinzie, and not the wumman."

Bryant rose up hastily and went forth to carry out the instructions of his master to the very letter.

Hardly was he gone when MacKenzie took up his rifle and went out to the woods for the same end and purpose, murmuring to himself.

"Rheinhardt, your days or mine are numbered."

CHAPTER XIV

HECTOR IS APPOINTED SENTINEL-GUARD OVER THE TRADERS' POST

As soon as the two intruders had been disposed of the Captain took charge and held the vessel in mid-stream, allowing it to drift down into the open waters of the bay. Both bays stood on either side of the helm, Hector relating to the Captain, as best he could, the events of the morning and the circumstances which led up to them. To this recital Conossoway was also an interested listener. Neither of the men could conceal their admiration for the part played by the boys and their pleasure in that Rheinhardt and his men had been so completely worsted.

As they reached the mouth of the river, there was descried a thin line of white smoke going skyward, the silent signal of an Indian that hid away behind the bushes a few rods from the shore, its inmates evidently up and about, though it was so early in the morning. To this spot the Captain ordered the schooner hauled.

"We must pull her in there," the Captain instructed as he pointed to a small inlet piercing the mainland at the farther end of which the tepee was erected.

Conossoway and the three boys entered the dinghy and with an oar apiece began hauling the vessel to the place suggested. After entering the mainland, the inlet swung to the left, forming a narrow elongated neck of water behind the tepee and parallel to the mainland. This place afforded not only shelter for the vessel, but served to hide it completely from view except to one standing on the rock immediately above. Into the inlet the schooner was towed as quietly as possible, but not quietly enough to leave undisturbed the dwellers within the tepee. These came out, a squaw and her daughter, a girl about sixteen years of age, who evidently did not appreciate the visit from this early in the morning. At the appearance of Conossoway their disquietude was quickly removed, and they were soon in animated conversation with them even before the schooner had made a landing.

Louis was the first to disembark. He snagged the vessel fore and aft, using the trees that grew up in the crevices of the rocks as tie-posts, after which the others followed him.

In conversation with the squaw, Captain Ike ascertained that her husband had left early that morning to join Rheinhardt's men in making an attack upon a tramp schooner which had appeared unexpectedly among them through the night, and which they were to attack at break of day if so be they found it unfriendly. The call came to him through the night from another Indian, an emissary of Rheinhardt.

Captain Ike in turn informed them of the discovery of MacGregor's skeleton and the capture of Mrs. MacGregor within the last few minutes and that probably her husband had a share in the capture.

The daughter, unlike so many Indian girls at her age, did not seem averse to conversation but smiled pleasantly when Louis enquiry if she heard any shooting.

"Not here, but over on the river. Maybe someone shooting duck."

"No, it was Rheinhardt's men chasing our boat."

"And who shoot?"

"That other boy," Louis pointed to Hector standing a little distance away, the Captain's rifle still in his hand.

"Kill any?" the squaw asked.

Louis shook his head, but said nothing.

Lifting her hand imprecatingly, the squaw addressing Charlie, though her eyes, sparkling with fire, were directed towards Hector.

"Dey kill MaGrigger, your fadder, dey steal your mudder. Shoot, boy, to kill. Shoot 'em here," she said as she placed her hand on her breast over her heart.

Hector shuddered as he saw the vehemence with which she urged the taking of life for life, as if it were not only a necessary experience, but a bounden duty under the circumstances.

The seriousness of the situation which was before them increased in magnitude as he contemplated the numerical strength and desperate characters whom they had need to face.

The effect on Conossoway was instantaneous. He spoke one word in their own language in answer to which the daughter ran into the tepee, and brought out a hunting knife, sheathed in a deerskin pocket attached to a girdle, and handed it to him. Conossoway took the proffered weapon, examined it, and then fastened the girdle around his body, the knife completely hidden from view but readily accessible when needed.

Thus equipped, "Come, boy," he said to Hector, and started into the woods in the direction of the trader's camp. Hector turned and followed, Charlie with him. He led the boys over the rocks and through the woods, along a rough path that zigzagged up the cliff which bounded the inlet on the north side. So steep and rough was it that the boys had to help each other at times in order to make the ascent in safety, while Conossoway climbs his way up as nimbly as a mountain goat.

When they reached the top, Hector, thoughtless, giving expression to his thought, or perhaps as an apology for their state of situation, exclaimed, "This is a mountain, trek."

"Liddle hill, dat's all," was the answer, which might mean that the boys were tender-feet, or that greater eminences than these might yet be expected before they were through with their explorations among the rocks of La Cloche.

With pitiless disregard of their stalking inexperience and their incapacity for endurance, Conossoway again struck forward. Choosing his way cautiously, he led them in a circuitous path around the brow of the hill until they came to a break in the thick underwood, and there he stood alert. Hector was amazed when he saw right immediately before them the camp of the trader with whom Conossoway expected to find Mrs. MacGregor, while over the top of the thickets that surrounded the opening they deserted the river, and the identical spot where he had spent the night before, the place where the events of the morning were so unexpectedly staged.

As a precaution against discovery, they prostrated themselves on the ground for the example and order of Conossoway to a sheltered spot on the brow of the rock which gave them a complete command of view of both the opposite shore of the river and the camp beside them. The Indian was setting himself out to make some discoveries of the whereabouts of the traders before proceeding further. Observing a crow fly and perch on the limb of a dead pine on the shore of the river, he gave the command to Hector:

"Shoot him, crow," as he pointed out it sat.

Hector threw his rifle into line; pulled the trigger; the crow fell.

"Oh!" exclaimed Charlie as he saw the quickness and accuracy with which he handled the rifle. Conossoway unmoved, kept his eyes fixed on the opposite shore. In a few minutes two men were seen running past an opening along the pathway that ran parallel to the bank, where they evidently were ambushed. Charlie now understood Conossoway's reasons for demanding an exhibit of Hector's skill. It was to detect whether Rheinhardt's men were still on the other side of the river, or were now an auxiliary force for the defence of the camp on this side of the river where he expected Mrs. MacGregor was being detained.

As soon as this discovery was made, turning to Hector as he adjusted his knife, he gave them a further inkling of his plans.

"I go; watch him door; if dey come out, shoot 'em."

He arose, stalked back into the wood, but presently emerged at the door of the camp. The boys saw him quietly enter in. Shortly after he came out, stood on the alert, peered up and down for a minute or two and then came back to the boys. The camp was tenantless. Conossoway was perplexed, and Charlie was cruelly disappointed when he saw the Indian return without his mother.

"Didn't you see anything of Mother?"

There was concern indicated in Charlie's voice as he asked this question of the Indian when he saw that he was volunteering for information concerning the results of the inspection of the traders' premises.

"Notinks," he jerked out abruptly.

"But how could they move out so soon?" enquired Hector. "Do you suppose they are hiding in the woods somewhere near us?"

To this Conossoway made no reply. He took out his pipe and lighting it continued in cut reverie.

"Cap'n Ike and me not nuff to fight all de traders; must be more Injuns."

This remark was addressed to no one in particular, though it summed up the train of thought that occupied his mind as he sat silently smoking his pipe. In fact he was planning the massacre of the whole camp, and only needed that the Captain should second his proposal, and he would at once set the undertaking in motion.

Hector realized that they were being drawn into an ugly situation, an escape from which providence alone could supply.

"What shall we do next?" he asked, when he saw that he was making no immediate movement to discover the whereabouts of Mrs. MacGregor. "Had we not better try and find where they are?"

"By'n bye, dey make dinner and then we make smoke."

"But that will be a long time yet. Is there any some other way of finding out where they are?"

Turning to Charlie, "You go, tell Cap'n Ike come," he instructed him.

"But will Charlie be able to find his way back alone? Don't you think you had better go with him and leave me here to do the watching until you all get back?" suggested Hector.

"You not 'fraid?"

"Afraid! Oh, no. Why should I be? There's One up there that takes care of me, Jack."

As Hector spoke, he pointed his hand skyward, indicating the source from which he expected protection.

"Maybe Missus MaGrigger, too?"

"Most certainly," was the ready answer of Hector.

Simultaneously with the finishing of this remark by Hector, there came floating down from far up in the sky the plaintive sound that he had heard over the inlet the day that he met the Indians who had set him adrift on the sea. In remote and desolate surrounding the call of the loon has not the unusual sound of producing a feeling of loneliness. To see the tenseness of feeling already aroused from the events of the morning caused it to produce in the minds of the three more than its usual effect. Strangely coincident that it should repeat this call three times as it passed over from the one lake to the other to which flying, once when approaching, a second time when over their heads, and a third time when it was some distance past.

"Three times, and Mrs. MaGrigger she not here," soliloquised Conossoway.

The significance of this remark was not lost on Charlie. He turned pale, and his lips quivered with emotion as his large gray eyes became surfaced with tears.

Seeing this Conossoway stood up erect and alert. "You no cry. If your mudder hurt, Cap'n and me kill de whole gang."

"Keep a brave heart," added Hector, "I have a feeling that this thing is going to come out alright yet."

The rescue of Mrs. MacGregor, or revenge, was the alternatives that Conossoway had it for himself.

"Watch the smoke, we back soon," were his instructions to Hector, while to Charlie he uttered one word in Indian in resolute command and stalked off.

"He wants me to go with him," Charlie explained, but at the same time protested his reluctance in leaving Hector alone in woods and in the immediate neighbourhood of an unscrupulous foe.

But Hector would hear of no objections to is going.

"Don't disappoint him. Follow him right up. I'm not the least bit nervous or afraid.

As a matter of fact, Hector felt himself buoyed up with a spirit of confidence, the reason for which he could not account, but such a hold had it upon his mind, that it seemed to be to him the more he needed help, the more buoyantly hopeful was his outlook on the future. Left alone, he began to spot for himself the best possible position that would serve the double purpose of his observation and seclusion.

"There is something in all this, whatever it may be," said he to himself—as he thought of the variety of circumstances which he had compelled to experience in so rapid an invasion during the past few days of his life.

The morning might have provided a wearied watch but for the variety of interests that surrounded him. All around, the leaves of the maple trees, those pinnated emblems of his native country, were dropping down one by one, carpeting the rocks about with their variegated colours. He gathered armfuls of them and, in the hollow where he lay, formed a comfortable bed for himself, where, lying with head and shoulders elevated, he commanded a full view of the river, on the banks of which he was expecting to see, soon, the traders come into view. Evergreens of all shades and sizes grew in thick groups on either shore of the river, and though there were occasional openings, these provided a sufficient screen to hide from his view the trader's place of concealment. Looking out over the scene before and around him, there was nothing within the immediate view which would give him any clue to the discovery of Mrs. MacGregor. He watched carefully every opening in the woods, but no one put in an appearance. The traders and their men had apparently drifted the scene of the morning's conflict.

In marked contrast to this apparent absence of human life, wild life manifested itself abundantly in the marsh grounds, towards the mouth of the river. It was the season of wild duck, and innumerable flocks were floating about in the shallow waters, while an equal number were hidden among the wild rice, many of whom had come down recently from the far north and had joined themselves to the native birds at this place, where was supplied them one of the best of places for a rendezvous, a feeding place as they journeyed southward in quest of their winter abode.

Hector watched their movements with interest, as tired of one place, or seeking food or variety in another, they would rise up to flocks, sometimes so large that he would be led to believe that they were getting ready to set out on another stage of their journey but after circling around, would alight again in a more favoured spot. One incident in this world of wild life occurred, destined to affect the fortunes of Hector, and bring about the close of his sentry duties.

"High up in the air, the "Honk, honk," of a flock of wild geese was heard. When they got directly above the marsh, he noticed the leader change its course, and soon the flock were circling around above Hector's head, coming down a little lower with every circle, apparently making observations with a view suitability of this sheltered inlet as a place of rest. So low at last did they fly above him that he could easily discern their shape and size. Involuntarily he took hold of his rifle. In other circumstances, he would have brought down their leader, but though greatly temped to do so in any case, .he knew this would be to disclose his presence to any traders who might be within near reach of him. With great regret he put his rifle back in its former position by his side, saying to himself as he did so, "The opportunity of a lifetime and I dare not lose it."

But if Hector refrained from shooting, not for another in his near presence. A few rods distant a shot was fired. A goose fell out of air and careered downward to the earth, falling at Hector's side. Simultaneously the flocks parted, and Hector found himself standing face to face before one of the traders with a rifle in his hand.

"Good morning!" said Hector gallantly and cheerfully, perhaps from force of habit or want of something better to say.

"The dickens to you, young fellow! What are you doing here?" the trader answered back with surprise and show of indignation.

"I am looking for Mrs. MacGregor," frankly replied Hector.

"Mrs. MacGregor!" the trader repeated in surprise. "And where is she?"

"She was taken off our boat and carried away by some of your men, I suppose."

The trader was evidently not displeased with Hector's openness and candor. Gazing at the youth, the hardness of his face relaxed, a studied expression passed over his countenance, a look of surprise study. "What is your name young fellow?" he next asked.

"Hector MacLeod."

"Hector MacLeod!" the man exclaimed. "Why that's my own name!"

"It is," answered Hector with eager excitement. "Then you must be my grandfather's younger brother,"

"That may or may not be. Where do live?"

"We live in New York, but my grandfather lives in Toronto."

"And what is your grandfather's name?"

"Lorne MacLeod. He used to sail a schooner on these lakes some years ago."

"And was your father's name Hector, or Hector Campbell?"

"Hector Campbell was his full name."

"Ay, ay," continued the man, "did you ever see your grandfather?"

"Yes, I was with him a few weeks before I came up here."

"Ay, ay, and your father was Hector Campbell MacLeod?"

"Yes."

"And how did you get up here?"

Hector related his experiences shortly, but with increased interest to the trader.

"What brought the schooner here, if you were making for the Bustard's?"

"We came in here for shelter. The two men had something to drink and they both went to sleep and left the care of the boat to the young Indian, Louis Conossoway."

"How many more men did you have with you?"

"We hadn't any."

"You hadn't? Then who did the shooting?"

"I suppose I did," answered Hector humbly and with a smile.

"Ay, and you hit one of Rheinhardt's men?"

"Perhaps so. I tried to cripple his hand when he had his gun in line for the Indian lad."

"And don't you know, lad, that 'Whose sheddeth man's blood, by man shall his blood be shed,' is the law on this lake." This the trader said with emphasis, which was intended without a doubt to put Hector aware that he was now an outlaw, and the Avenger of Blood would await the opportunity when he would have to pay the full penalty with his life.

After this remark the trader looked down on the ground with a studied expression, every now and then breaking the silence with the same two words, "ay, ay" After a while he looked up and said, "Hector, you'll come with me to-day," with a note of sympathy to the word Hector, "and seeing as you have drawn blood, you'd better keep a lookout on the trees, for there might be a gun behind one them."

Hector made no answer.

"And was your father a good shot?" further enquired the trader.

"Yes, it was he who taught me to shoot."

"Ay, ay," again he repeated, and took a seat on the rock boulder behind which Hector had been lying concealed on the lookout for Mrs. MacGregor. As he did so, he observed the rusted revolver lying on the ground among the leaves, which Hector had found in the cache. Immediately he asked, with a quick jerky tone of voice, "Where did you get that?"

"I got it in a cave where I stayed the night before last."

"You did?" The trader reached down, pick up the weapon and examined it carefully. Every chamber was still full.

"That's MacGregor's, I would know it anywhere."

"It's just the same as I got it," explained Hector.

"And where did you get it? The question was asked as by one who had been told and forgotten.

"In the cache, on the island where I was marooned," answered Hector.

"That was MacGregor's cache, lad. He did some trading for me on the lake, but disappeared. You wouldn't hear anything about him, I suppose?"

"Yes, I found the skeleton bones of a man buried on the island. The skull bone was fractured, and Captain Ike said it was MacGregor's."

"Ay, poor fellow. There'll be a day of reckoning for the man who did it, and I think I know him."

"There were two men came there the night I was there."

"And where you alone?"

"Yes. They came there towards morning."

131

"And what did they do?"

"They ran away when they saw me, but I heard what they said."

"Ay, ay. Rheinhardt's men. It wasn't Rheinhardt himself, do you think?"

"There was a third man on the sail boat or canoe. He seemed to be the man who was doing the ordering around."

With this the trader rose up quickly, picked up the fallen goose, and turning to Hector, said, "If you are the MacLeod that I think you are, then it was Heaven who sent you here to-day."

There was something about this stranger which, from the very first, won Hector's confidence, and with a trust begotten by this judgment, he rose up immediately and followed him.

CHAPTER XV

THE ARRIVAL OF' AN AUXILIARY FIGHTING FORCE

The events of the fatal morning of conflict had come down upon Mrs. MacGregor in such quick succession, that she had not time to realize their significance until she found herself being forcibly carried away from the vessel by Rheinhardt's men.

She was dropped by the two who boarded the boat into a waiting canoe manned by four Indians, seized and held in the centre by one of them, while the other three paddled hurriedly up the river, skirting its right bank. They continued paddling energetically until they came to the Gorge. At the head of the portage, they disembarked, and the steerman who was their spokesman to her on every occasion, in fairly good English ordered her to step out. Starting out along the portage trail and following one another closely in a single file, she was ordered to take the nearest place to the rear. After a little, the leader turned to the right into the woods, followed by the others. Mrs. MacGregor, seeing that she was being led into a thick woods, refused to follow them any further.

At this, the Indians began to threaten her, and show an ugly temper. "You not walk; we carry."

"Why do you Indians obey Rheinhardt, and do this kind of work for him?" she asked of them, trying in this way to dissuade them from their undertaking. "Rheinhardt is not the Indian's friend; MacGregor was the Indian's friend; so is MacLeod; so is Rory MacKenzie. I'll give you a hundred dollars to take me back to the vessel, to Captain Ike and Jack Conossoway. It's all I've got, but I'll give it all, if you'll do that."

This in fact, was her total earnings for her summer's work as a teacher of a private school for girls in Toronto. She had set it apart for Charlie, to help him up another rung in the ladder of his education.

"If we could only lift him up and make the stand on an equal footing with Lester's boy's. I would be content to die," she had written to her husband, as they struggled together to give him a generous education.

This was her one great ambition for her son. Lester was her younger brother, and she, his only living sister, but now with her older brother, disowned of the family. In her marriage she had followed the voice of her heart, but not their judgment, which was that she had married beneath herself and must be punished for it.

"Let her swelter under her self-chosen life," her father had decreed, as he handed over all of his wealth to this son only, Ignoring any claims which Frances her older brother, now somewhere in America, might have upon his property.

And this, too, was the destiny that Lester and his family desired for her as themselves luxuriated in comforts, not of their men achieving, but the legacy derived from the unyielding father's will.

In other days the spirit of a proud mother would bend at Christmas time, and Franny would receive a remembrance of a love that once had been hers. Now, this too was poor. The author of this yearly kindness had too lowed the great procession, and her body lay crumbling into dust, in that far-off land of silences, from which no kindness nor message ever comes. She struggled upward with her boy, to lift him up, not to the aristocracy of wealth, but the aristocracy of an educated man of affairs.

This ambition of Mrs. MacGregor, her husband, during his life-time, strongly supported. In the hard years immediately following the close of the Napoleonic war, they lived on the ragged edge of poverty. Notwithstanding he was a man of education and parts, he could obtain no employment in his active land. Determined that he would obtain for his wife and child that place in life to which they were entitled, he made up his mind to emigrate to Canada, where opportunities for trade and achievement were scattered everywhere throughout the length and breadth of the country. He obtained employment in Montreal as a draughtsman. Although the wages to him at first seemed satisfactory, and would have been if living conditions were the same in that city as in the Old Country, yet when he came face to face with the expenditures demanded of him in his new environment, he found that his savings were wholly inadequate for the requirements of his wife and child at home. To better his circumstances, for he was a man of daring, initiative and adventure, he struck out into the woods to become a frontiersman and a trader of furs among the Indians. He became partner with two others, MacKenzie and MacLeod, who organized themselves into a firm of independent traders, agents in fact, of the North West Fur Company at the Espanola, with their headquarters at La Cloche. From that time onward his earning mounted steadily upward, until his great fortune reached its climax in the discovery of a rich copper mine lying in a north eastward direction from their trading post.

The claim, in fact was the discovery of his partner, Hector MacLeod, but this wealthy man, knowing of his partner's circumstances and ambitions, passed the ownership of it over to MacGregor.

"Take it, Claire," he said. ":If you can make anything out of it, you are greatly welcome to it. I know several other prospects equally as good, and one of these days I'll stake out another for myself."

It was not long until a buffalo corporation offered him a princely sum for the claim. He consulted MacLeod immediately.

"Take it," his partner counseled, "and get back to your wife and child. This life in the woods may be all right for a bachelor like me, but for you, with a home and boy, don't miss the chance of comfort and happiness which their offer gives you."

It is needless to say that Claire Butler promptly accepted this counsel of wisdom, and immediately disposed of his claim. In the meantime, Hector MacLeod struck out northward to the Hudson Bay district, and was lost to La Cloche and its environment for the short period, as the woodsmen count time, of six years.

There, even to that far north, rumour reached him of foul play at the La Cloche and the visit to it afterwards of Mrs. Butler and her son looking for information of her husband and finding none. Believing the well founded, Hector MacLeod came back determined to mete out justice to whomever justice was due.

The offer by Mrs. MacGregor to buy up the Indians seemed to have had some influence on their movements. They sat down on the ground in a group around herm giving her an opportunity for a further effort to save herself from a fate, the nature of which she had no way of discovering.

"Who sent you over to the schooner this morning?" she asked.

"Rheinhardt," their spokesman answered.

"And why?"

"To fight the boat and get Mrs. MacGregor."

"Is he paying you to do this?"

"Yeh, he promised whiskey."

"Is he a greater friend of yours than MacLeod?"

"Rheinhardt gives whiskey; MacLeod he says "No.""

"I'll give you a bottle. I have one on the boat, if you take me back there."

This offer had more influence upon the dusky captors, than had her previous offer of money. She might have succeeded to arguing her liberty through it, but at that moment rifle shots were heard, some in succession, other concurrent, which led the Indians to the unanimous belief that another fight was being staged. Jumping up quickly, they seized her and led her off forcibly into the woods. Coming to a Cedar swamp, situated at the foot of a bluff of rock, known as Fox Bluff, they circled round it and came back along the foot of the bluff, until they reached a little hut completely screened from view by the rock on one side and the thick woods on the other. Opening the door, they forced her in, and then closed it securely, barring it from the outside.

Left alone, she threw herself down on an improvised berth, and gave vent to her feelings in tears of disappointment. All her efforts towards the realization of the ambition of her life, the education of her son, the lifting of his head on par with Lester's boys, seemed to be made futile, first by the loss of her husband, and now by the machinations of a villainous whiskey-trader. 'Why did nature had find fight against her?' she queried, in the bitterness of her spirit and hopelessness of her imprisonment.

For the time being she was willing to acquiesce in the faith of that infidel philosopher, who in his quest for the highest good, concluded that the greatest was never to have been born at all, and the next best to that, to die young.

Her own troubles were sufficient to have broken her spirit into hopeless despair, but there was the added burden, the uncertainty concerning the schooner and the boys. She observed with gladness as she was being paddled away from the vessel, that Conossoway had risen to the occasion, and was apparently giving a good account of himself. She observed, also, that the shooting had ceased. Was it because Hector was disarmed or because he had succeeded in vanquishing their antagonists? Fervently she prayed for their safety, a religious exercise which to us reflex influence upon her mind, begot to her a spirit of confidence, ending in a calm which enabled tired nature to rest itself in sleep.

In the meantime, the events at the trader's quarters were moving rapidly forward to a fateful ending. When Conossoway and Charlie arrived back at the tepee, they found Captain Ike pacing up and down the shore in restless mood.

"What luck, Jack?" he enquired, as soon both appeared before him.

"All gone," answered Jack.

"Didn't you see anyone?"

Jack shook his head negatively.

"Then we're off to the Bustards right away. The fishermen must have their goods, and this is no hole to be hanging around in, with their summer's wages on the boat."

"Maybe tomorrow," answered Jack. Then, sitting down, he unfolded his plan for the extermination of the gang. He found a ready seconder in the Captain, but it would be after their return from the Bustards, not before.

He was too sane to be caught facing an unscrupulous gang, now chafing for revenge, without a sufficient number of helpers. He would hasten to the Bustards, and with the hard help of a dozen fisher-folk Indians, support alike in the use of the rifle and the knife, would stage a fight to the finish, as he intimated to Charlie.

"But dat boy, we leave him in de bush," remarked Jack, as he discussed their contemplated trip.

"Well, get him, then, and let's go away,"

"Me no go, Captain Ike. Dat boy in de bush an' dat Missus Magrigger, she call me. No, Captain Ike. P'raps to-morrow, but not to-day."

"Then, if not you, it's Charlie," he snapped out in reply. "What say you boy? Is it you and Louis for the Bustards?"

To the amazement of both of them, Charlie answered unhesitatingly: "If you wish it, Captain, and you promise to come back right away."

His answer was a surprise, because they certainly expected he would refuse, had there were two reasons which weighed with him, leading him to this decision. He knew that it would be better that he should go than the Indian, because, if his mother was to be liberated, Conossoway was the most capable person to do it. Besides this, he felt they must have more help, and the Captain's solution to get these from the Bustards well away, seemed the right one. Hence, the readiness in assenting to go.

The Captain looked pleased on receiving his answer. Forgetful of the trying experiences of the morning and observing how pale he was, he concluded that it was due to lack of food. Turning abruptly to the Indian woman, now standing in the doorway of the tepee listening to their conversation, and with more directness and less politeness than is usual, he enquired:

"Say, Squaw, have you anything to eat in there?"

"Yeh, plentee."

"Give some to the boy."

Waving Charlie ahead, and Louis following, the Captain went into the wigwam and took his seat with the others on the raised platform on the right side of the camp. The Indian woman, raking among the hot ashes under the fire in the centre, brought out some well roasted potatoes, and with them, some fish cooked in clay jackets kept there in readiness, and she handed out to each a generous supply.

"Dat boy, he not have any," interpolated Jack, as he devoured the food set aside as his portion. He was still thinking of Hector alone in the woods. On mention of this, the Indian woman raked the ashes again, and discovered to them all that the last of her supply was not yet exhausted.

"Conossoway, you'll have to get something to him right away," the Captain ordered. "It'll never do to let that lad lie out there and get weak with hunger. He must be fed, and fed good, if he's going to meet these fellows in another fight."

A gentle breeze had arisen and it was blowing favourably for their journey, so Captain Ike, with Charlie and Louis as his crew—the wife of Conossoway was still in the hold asleep—set sail with the schooner for the Bustards. As it ploughed its way through the waters towards its destination, no incident occurred to attract their interest until they had made some considerable distance on the journey. Charlie, looking westward, observed a mackinac to their right. It was not long until he observed it change its course and bear down in their direction.

"A sail to our right, Captain. It seems to be heading towards us."

"It might be that," the Captain answered slowly, as he watched the direction in which it was heading.

The schooner did not slacken speed, but yet the mackinac was moving at a more rapid rate than they were.

"The wind is to their advantage, Charlie, but we'll give them a run if it's a trader," the captain remarked as he observed it approaching nearer.

"That's a strange sail in these waters Charlie," was his added remark, when it had come sufficiently near for them to discern its appearance and its occupants. "It looks to me like Rusty Brown's old mackinac. Slow up, Charlie, we'll see what they want. Yes, it's Rusty," he repeated later with assurance.

"When they had come within hearing distance of his voice, he called out, "Hello, there, Rusty. What are You doing fishing in these waters?"

"Hello, there, Captain Ike! Have you seen anything of the two Indians, Little Knife and Wagoosh around since you came up?'

"No, but I picked up a lad the same kind of those three you have there, a fellow by the name of Hector MacLeod."

At the mention of this, the three boys gave a shout, for they were none other than Alan, Lorne and Wilfred.

"Was he alive?" asked Alan.

"Alive!. Why, of course he was. What would I do with a dead corpse?"

"Where is he now?"

"Up the shore along with the whiskey-traders—Rheinhardt and the rest of them you know them better'n I do, Rusty."

"Did the traders steal him?" asked Lorne, for as yet they had no knowledge of the circumstances which led to his disappearance.

"Not they, not at any rate when we left, whatever they've done since. Good shot, isn't he, Rusty?"

"The boys say he is."

"Well, he's up there in the bush with my rifle, and he's been trying his hand on some of the traders, and I'm afraid he's in for a rough time if they set their eyes on him."

"But how did he get there?"

"We picked him up on an island shore yesterday night and some of the whiskey he had with him."

"Whiskey!" they all exclaimed together

"Yes, he found some of MaGrigger's down on an island where he camped after he got out of the water, and I found him there, sitting on the shore with MaGrigger's bones, and took him for a trip with me up the lake. I left him back there with the Indians to do a little watching until I get back. The gang ran off this morning with this boy's mother," and he pointed to Charlie, "and Conossoway and he are gone to bring her back. There was some tall shooting going on when we left a few hours ago, and it may be he's got them or they've got him."

"But why should the boy get mixed up with the traders?" asked Rusty.

"He likes shooting, and the shooting was good this morning, so he tried his hand on Rheinhardt and his gang."

"But there must have been some cause. The boy wouldn't start shooting at human beings without a reason."

"Reason? Why, Rheinhardt lost his temper as he always does, and began choking this boy, and the other boy got behind the goods and began to shake him off with his gun. Conossoway and I were asleep and the boys had it all to themselves and were getting along to a fine finish when some of Rheinhardt's men came from the other side and got on the boat. They carried off the boy's mother; if it wasn't for that the boys would have won the day."

"But Hector didn't shoot any man?" asked Alan with concern.

"Didn't, eh? I guess he did, and he'll have to do some more yet if he comes out of that bush with a whole skin on him."

"Can you tell us where he is?" asked Alan with anxious concern.

"At the La Cloche, or somewhere in the bush round about there. You'll find him all right, for he's a good shot and has the best rifle on the Bay. The rifle with the longest range and the best man behind it wins the day," answered the Captain.

"This is a stiff breeze that's getting up and there is an appearance of a sea coming," Rusty remarked, as he observed the size of the waves increasing.

"It's here already, Rusty. What do you think of those fellows?" he pointed to the rollers, white-peaked, moving along in quick succession one after another towards the shore. "Yes, Rusty, you'd better get along and give a hand to save the boy and the lad's mother. You know the nest."

"Ay."

"Well, pull in on this side. There's an Indian tepee behind the ridge. Stay there until someone comes and they'll put you on right track to do the rest."

The captain was elated at the turn events had taken. "Four more helpers and all white folk. At this rate we'll not need any Injuns," he thought. "I'd rather tie their hands and feet with basswood thongs and send the whole gang to jail. It would be more fun and last longer," and once more the hearty laugh of the Captain was heard as he thought of Rheinhardt and his men brought under grip of the law.

The arrival of Rusty Brown with the three boys induced Captain Ike to change his ground in respect to the trip to the Bustards. Turning around, he followed the mackinac back to the Indian tepee.

They were all experienced seamen, and notwithstanding the roughness of the weather, it was not long until the two vessels were occupying the cove which sheltered the schooner in the morning.

Rusty Brown and the boys began forth with to prepare their encampment in early readiness for the night, but Captain Ike and Charlie strolled off to ascertain, if possible further clues concerning the day and its happenings.

CHAPTER XVI

TOMB OF FLORA MACLEAN AND HER HUSBAND

On their way back to the lodge, the trader continued questioning Hector concerning his family.

"Your father will be a young man, I suppose?"

"In his prime, I should judge," answered Hector.

"And he will be having brothers?"

"No, we are the only MacLeods of the second generation that are left."

"Ay, ay," he repeated, "the only MacLeods left. And did they know you came here?"

"Oh, no, I got lost in the bush," and here Hector recounted his conversation with his grandfather, and all of his experiences which he had passed through since the storm.

The trader was visibly affected. He quoted to himself almost inaudibly, the well known text, "Who knoweth but thou hast come to the Kingdom for such a time as this," a passage of scripture so familiar to the Highlanders that it was to them a constant inspiration, fortifying them to courage in the undertaking of many hard tasks. Then turning to Hector, he said:

"Your chums, I hope to see them soon, If I get through with to-morrow."

"What's on for to-morrow?" asked Hector innocently.

"Rheinhardt or I is to pass across," asserted his uncle coolly, "blood for blood, and although I am not the next of kin, yet his punishment cannot be any longer delayed."

MacLeod was one of those peculiar type of men, the greater injury done to him, the slower he was to move in his own defense. Yet let him make the start in the directions required for his own vindication, and there was nothing, humanly speaking, which could hinder him from carrying it out to its completed end. He had come from the north, so did MacKenzie with him, to demand retribution from Rheinhardt. Of a mystical temperament, he had concluded that since his nephew had been brought there, through circumstances not of his own choosing, it must be in order to perform some service to his family, of which himself was the alone representative in the woods of La Cloche. During the weeks that had passed since MacKenzie and he had turned their faces southward, he had a premonition of an impending fate. The discovery, so unexpectedly and under such peculiar circumstances, of a representative of his own blood, provided the means by which a cherished desire of his life would be realized. This desire he would reveal to Hector in due course, and then await the trend of events and their ultimate issue.

On their arrival at the bank of the river, they met an Indian and a white man.

"B'jou, B'jou," Hector's uncle saluted cheerfully.

The approaching Indian answered with a like cheerfulness, as did also the white man, until Hector unnoticed before, came under their observation. At the sight of him, both the Indian and the white man stood and stared with astonishment.

"What's up?" asked Hector's uncle sharply.

"Who's that fellow with you?" the white man asked, for he recognized Hector as one of the occupants of the schooner in the morning

"Why, this is my nephew, my grandnephew," answered MacLeod.

The Indian and MacLeod began to speak to each other in the Indian tongue. Hector did not understand the subject of conversation, but saw his uncle become greatly agitated.

"These men say that Rheinhardt and MacKenzie had a quarrel a few minutes ago and that a duel is to be fought between them to-morrow, Hector."

This information he imparted after the other two had taken their departure, which was hastened by the echo of a rifle shot which rang out on the far side of the river, followed almost simultaneously by another. The restless agitated look of the white man took up and then an increased excitement of further delay.

"Let's move on," he instructed his Indian companion, "we have no time standing here."

"What can they mean?" remarked Hector. After the two of them had disappeared. "Did you observe how excited the white man got after he heard that shot?"

"There is something in the wind, and the Indian is hired to carry it out," answered the uncle. "It may be you, or it may be someone else they are after. We will follow them in a little down the path and see which way they go."

Here the rock rose up in gradual slope' forming a slight plateau at the top. As they walked along the path on which the two men preceded them, Hector looked up to survey the appearance of the Bluff, when to his surprise, he observed under the cliff, sitting behind a clump of trees, the white man and his companion lying there prone. Was it deer or human beings for which they were on the lookout?

"See," said Hector, as he pointed them out to his Uncle.

The Indian made, as it were, to draw himself a little closer behind the grove of closely growing underwood behind which he was hiding when he saw that he was observed. MacLeod, however, shouted at him to come down, using, of course, the Indian language. The Indian readily obeyed.

From him, he elicited the information that both he and the white man were sent by Rheinhardt on the lookout for MacKenzie, but would not admit whether or not they meditated bodily injury to him.

Immediately he received this information, MacLeod ordered the two to accompany them to his lodge, so that he might acquaint MacKenzie, in their presence, of the conspiracy hatched against him.

When they arrived there, to the astonishment of both of them, Captain Ike and Charlie were there before them, awaiting the appearance of MacKenzie, who had not yet returned from his visit to Rheinhardt.

"You got back last night, Mac," Captain Ike began, when their mutual salutations were over?

"Yes, been away six years, Captain Ike, six years, and they only seem like six days."

"Been up at the Hudson, eh?"

"Yes, east and west and all over. I don't suppose there's a river between here and there, we didn't navigate."

"Lots of fur, eh?"

"Ay, ay, but better than either, mines. The Country is full of them, Captain Ike."

"Still at your old tricks, Mac, eh?"

"The same old game, Captain. Anything new at La Cloche?"

"Nothing. I suppose you heard Magrigger went across."

This he said without regard to Charlie's presence, who was hearing again the Captain's version of his father's death.

"Ay, ay, some more of Rheinhardt's work, I suppose?"

"Rheinhardt says it was MacKenzie, but we know different."

"MacKenzie?"

"Yes, MacKenzie killed him for his money and his claim, he says. The Frenchies never came back either."

"And didn't you get any trace of them?"

"Last night for the first, Mac. That lad of yours," and he pointed to Hector, "found the bones on the island. He wanted me to take them with me, but I wasn't going to cross the Gap after night with any dead Man's bones on board, even if they were MaGrigger's."

"How did you come to know he was killed then, if you hadn't found him?"

"When MaGrigger's boat went out, you'll remember, Rheinhardt's went out after Rheinhardt's came back but not the Frenchies, and me and Conossoway have put two and two together ever since, and the more we think, the more we are sure what happened. This lad found him buried and he scraped up the bones and put them together and made a man of them. Then he gathered them up and put them in a basket. They are in the old cave now. You know the place, Mac."

"But who buried him? Rheinhardt would n't, I'm sure."

"It was Rusty. They were disturbed Rusty, Little Knife and Conossoway went after them. Seems Rusty got suspicious somehow, and yanked down the bay, but the bird got away. I don't think he got the money but Jack didn't know that. I wanted Jack to get the boy off last night, but he wouldn't go, no siree, and I think myself, 'He's afraid of the ghost of MaGrigger.' It's the old cache, all right, and the bottles and biscuits are there as MaGrigger left them."

"Ay, ay," was all the answer of the trader.

"Have you met the Missus, Mac?" the Captain asked, changing quickly the subject of their conversation. "Came with the boat last night. Was up here once afore looking for MaGrigger or his money, but she saw only Rheinhardt, and now he's got her over in his caboose there somewhere. That's her youngster there," and he pointed to Charlie.

"Hers! Stand up boy, till I see you," requested MacLeod.

Charlie stood as if he were a pupil in the public school, under the authority of his teacher. The trader looked at him earnestly for a time.

"Is he a MaGrigger, Mac?"

"Hardly, favours his mother's side. Looks more like his uncle, Rusty, but that other boy is a MacLeod, a pure MacLeod. I would know he was a MacLeod if I met him in Mexico."

"Captain Ike eyed Hector scrutinizingly, and there dawned upon his not altogether perfect observing powers somewhat of a resemblance between these two—the colour of their eyes, their hair, their physique, the one developed, the other moving onward in the same direction. To a keen observer, the resemblance would be striking, but to his dull mentality, it was only a possibility.

"Anything to you, Mac?" he asked, as this resemblance manifested itself to him.

"He will be if anybody touches him with so much as a little finger," he answered with a determination of purpose which meant the complete safeguarding of Hector's future movements from any display of animosity which the morning's combat and its results had brought him.

"But this doesn't settle our business Captain Ike. To-day the protection of the woman we'll leave in the hands of God. To-morrow it will be ours. Today you'll go back to Devil's island, and find out all that you can. To-morrow it's the end of Rheinhardt, or I haven't come back from the marsh without a. reason. To-day Hector and I we be together. The rest of you will have to go to your work without us."

"There's the pork and the flour, Mac. We'll have to look after that."

"Leave it with the fisher-folk if you want to. There's plenty of time to do both."

Captain Ike arose immediately to put his day's work into execution, beckoning to Charlie to follow. As he moved towards the door, he remarked, "That boy hasn't had anything to eat to-day yet, Mac, and its now past noon, I'm thinking."

It was a never-to-be-forgotten afternoon Hector which spent that day, with Lieutenant MacLeod, for this was none other than his long lost uncle. One event, however, of that afternoon stood out above all the rest in the after years of his memory

"You'll be going with me, Hector, to the foot of the La Cloche. We'll take the canoe to the Sault du Nouailles, and there make the portage. After that we'll cross the lake and from there through the woods. It is there I buried Flora. I'll be telling you about her when we get there."

When they arrived at the place Hector observed stones lying in a promiscuous heap, in no way different, apparently, from many Others scattered around at the foot of the mountain. No passer-by could deem what was hidden behind them. One by one, this stones were removed carefully by Lieutenant MacLeod. The last of them was a large slab sitting on its edge, and closing, what was in reality, the mouth of a cavern cut into the rock, not by human skill, but nature's own Handiwork. When this was removed there was revealed in the cavern, lying side by side; two barked and polished logs, the trunks of a large oak tree. On the one was carved the word "Flora"; on the other, "Hector." The soldier stood before it with a bared head. He lifted the cleft slab, which made up the cover of the one which bore his own name, and showed to Hector the tree hallowed out carefully, making it a fit casket for the dead.

"I have made Rusty promise, and Conossoway and Little Knife promise, and I want you to promise, that it is there the body of Hector Campbell MacLeod shall lie in his last long sleep."

The request was no sooner made, than Hector, his heart moved by mystic was pledged himself to its fulfillment.

"I promise, uncle," he repeated in a purposeful voice, which convinced Lieutenant MacLeod that the promise made would be kept unbroken.

"I can trust you, Hector," was the Uncle's responsive acceptance, "A MacLeod has never yet been known who was a traitor to his family."

There under the shadow of the LaCloche Hector listened to the life story of Flora MacLean, and the subsequent wanderings of that scion of a noble family, among the rivers and rocks of the great lone Northland, exploring with a faith the riches of its mineral resources, but accompanied always by the spirit of one, the memory of whose love and purity never left nor forsook him.

On their way home, when they arrived at the Sault du Nouailles, it was necessary that they should either make a portage, or do what before had never been attempted by Indian or white man—shoot the rapids.

The sun was getting low and they had a considerable distance yet to go before they would arrive home. Lieutenant MacLeod was anxious to reach there before nightfall. The shooting of the rapids would save them many minutes. At other times, he might have hesitated, realizing that discretion is always the better part of valour, but now a species of recklessness had taken possession of him. He was agitated, not only by arrival of his nephew, but by the multiplicity of other events which were making La Cloche, at this time, their place of concentration. Events never come singly, but on this clay they were following one another, and coming together, in hurricane rapidity. His spirit seemed to rise in consonance, and he felt himself equal to undertaking the impossible.

"Would you like to shoot the gorge?" he asked Hector, when the desire to do so seized his mind.

"Nothing would suit me better," answered Hector, as he looked down the swift-flowing chute and pictured on the retina of his imagination their canoe rapidly carried down over its boiling waters.

"Then we'll make the trial," replied his uncle, suiting the action to the word.

The canoe was started down with Hector. at the bow, while his uncle took the more important place of steersman at the stern. When they reached the tumbling waters of the Gorge, all attempts to direct the course of the canoe were futile. The swift flowing stream had taken matters in its own hand.

Their frail bark took a leap over the chute and they were momentarily expecting that the suction of the water at the foot would pull them under. With a powerful stroke by Hector at the bow, and with an equally expert movement at the same time, on the part of his uncle at the stern, the canoe veered to the left, carried forward by one of the currents to the opposite shore. There it

appeared as if it were going to strike head-on against a rock, but instead, it circled quickly round and round for a few moments, until MacLeod and his nephew had the craft again in their control. They had made an experiment and were triumphant. The success of this foolhardy undertaking filled the mind of Lieutenant MacLeod with cheerful enthusiasm.

"The fates are on our side, Hector," he repeated to his nephew, as they pulled out into the current of the river and safety.

"A canoe to our left, uncle." Hector observed.

"Yes, four in it, and all paddling swiftly, they are good strokes all of them," his relative answered.

"I believe they are pulling over this way," Hector further remarked as he watched their manoeuvers.

"Ease up and we'll see what they want."

Both ceased paddling. On their near approach, Hector could hardly believe his eyes or keep his excitement under control, for there without doubt were Rusty Brown and the three boys. It was a. joyous meeting, their measure of gladness only diminished by the untoward circumstances which seemed to envelop the trading-post on this particular day.

The twilight was deepening until the shadows of the trees were no longer visible in the waters when the two canoes reached the traders' lodge. MacLeod, seeing the Indians and the men of the post gathered in groups at the shore, awaiting their arrival sensed that something was wrong. At the head of the Indiana stood Louis Conossoway.

"What's up, boys?" enquired MacLeod.

"Rory has disappeared," one of them answered.

"Disappeared? Surely you fellows never allowed that Rheinhardt to commit another Crime."

Rusty Brown on landing would fain have expressed his apparent delight to Hector in the fortunate termination of their quest for him, but that service was monopolized by the three boys who crowded around him with affectionate enthusiasm, plying him with a chorus of questions, interspersed with expressions of amazing surprise and delight that they had stumbled so unexpectedly that afternoon upon him. Not much less delightful to Rusty was his meeting with Lieutenant MacLeod after his six years' separation from him. These two had much to discuss and plan, for, as already observed, the purpose of his return carried with it a matter of serious import in which Rusty Brown was also vitally concerned. The absence of MacKenzie on the eve of these grave undertakings and the kidnapping of Mrs. MacGregor by Rheinhardt added to the gravity of the situation. Rusty Brown had therefore much to hear and to tell, and Lieutenant MacLeod was in the mood to listen to any counsel that would help mete out justice to one whom he deemed had already too long escaped deserved punishment for his crimes.

CHAPTER XVII

THE RESCUE

After a short respite in troubled sleep, Mrs. MacGregor awoke in timid fear of the consequences which were to befall her. She looked round the hut, but there was nothing which would enable her to make her escape, or anything which she could use as a weapon of defence, should the need of such in any emergency be required. At any rate, she was too unnerved for any strenuous activity. Her hope was striving hard to dispel the spirit of gloom which now pervaded her mind. She prayed with fervour that she might be delivered from the power of Rheinhardt, a man whom she knew to be a slave of passion, so uncontrolled that it would drive him to any length to gain its end.

As she prayed, she was startled to hear someone removing the bars on the outside of the door. Her whole body trembled with fear. When it opened, what was her surprise to see a young Indian woman instead of the one whom her fears predicted.

"The sent of the Lord!" she exclaimed, on seeing her. After taking a seat by her side the young woman opened a parcel and displayed some food, a broiled partridge and some bread, and invited her to eat.

"Where's Captain Ike and the schooner?" she asked.

"Gone to Bustards," was the answer.

"And Charlie?"

"Gone too."

"And the other lad?"

"Me not know, somewhere in bush, Jack say."

"And Jack?"

"In bush, too, lookin' for boy but: see him nowhere."

"And the traders, where are they?"

"Up the river."

"Up the river?"

"Yeh, at Rheinhardt's post. Me see dem go in canoe. Maybe dey fight some more.

"Did you see them go?"

"Yeh, Rheinhardt go in canoe and then MacKenzie follow like mad."

"Where are you living?" she asked the young Indian.

"Wigwam on shore dere," she answered as she pointed in the direction of the bay where the schooner took shelter in the morning.

"You , alone?"

"Ma mudder and fadder dere, too, but dey gone out look, maybe they see boy too."

"Did anyone send you to look for me?"

"Fadder, he say you offer bottle and money,"

"I see. Was he one of the four who took me here this morning?"

"Yeh, and he not tell Rheinhardt me come."

"And Jack Conossoway, where is he?"

"Jack stay to look for you, and Cap'n Ike he go for more Injuns."

"What for?"

"Fight de traders."

"Oh dear! Was he drunk?"

"Ugh, not drunk, just mad."

After some further conversation, the Indian girl informed Mrs. MacGregor that it would be unsafe for them to stay there any longer, as Rheinhardt and his men might appear at any moment. She urged her to leave at once that she might lead her through the woods to the bank of a small stream, where was awaiting them, the Indian and his wife, with their canoe to bring her back in safety to Captain Ike's schooner.

The Indian girl led Mrs. MacGregor through the unpatched woods until they made a considerable distance eastward. On reaching the summit of a ridge that ran parallel with the river, they came to a trail leading them southward to the open waters of the bay. At this juncture both of the women were startled by hearing footsteps and seeing the underwoods sway as someone was making his way through them. Mrs. MacGregor drew herself timidly over by the side of the Indian girl, and clung to her arm, "Oh, say, is that some one behind us? She asked in a trembling whisper.

"Yeh, me hear," answered her companion not in the least perturbed.

"Do you think there is someone following us?"

"Yeh, me see man."

Mrs. MacGregor's fears would not permit her to look behind though both of them walked on assured they were being followed. If the Indian girl knew the identity of their pursuer, she did not disclose any information or make any further remarks concerning the incident. Both walked on hurriedly and in silence. Soon the open waters of the bay came in sight, and on the shore, Mrs. MacGregor observed an Indian and a squaw squatted beside their canoe.

"Is that your father?" she enquired, now relieved by the sight of them.

"Yeh, me fadder and me mudder."

Mrs. MacGregor felt herself unburdened of a great weight, when she saw her rescuers so near at hand, and two of them of her own sex.

"Oh, girl, how kind you have been to me!" she exclaimed. "If I could only repay you in some way I would gladly do it."

The two had reached the canoe a few minutes before the man following them appeared.

When he came up to them, "Frances, have you forgotten me?" he asked Mrs. MacGregor, as he put out his hand in cordial friendship to her.

"Can it be—it must be—Major MacKenzie," she answered with surprised delight.

"Yes, Frances, you are right. I stumbled on your whereabouts through one of the Indians and got there just as you were leaving. I did not know whether the girl with you was a friend or another of Rheinhardt's willing slaves?"

"A friend in need, Major. She has been an angel from God to me to-day."

"Don't fear any more, Frances. We'll look after you from this out."

Turning to the Indian, MacKenzie entered into conversation with him in his own language, among other things informing him he would be well paid for the services he had rendered in securing Mrs. MacGregor's release.

They all five entered the canoe and reached the Indian tepee as the twilight was beginning to fade away into night. The air was chill, and MacKenzie suggested to the Indian that he build a fire for their comfort. Before this fire, on the outside at the entrance to the wigwam, they sat discussing bygone days, but chiefly the tragic close of Claire's, her husband's, career. Their experiences together in the woods, the discovery of copper and silver mines, the sale of MacGregor's property to a Buffalo firm, and the rumour of foul play, MacKenzie reviewed them all to his interested listener. He assured her that notwithstanding the crime, the wealth he accumulated was still intact.

"There is one man on the bay you will be greatly pleased when you meet him. He it is has who has charge of your husband's money."

"Is that Lieutenant MacLeod?"

"No, not he, but another just as good."

"What's his name?"

"Rusty Brown is his name here, but his real name is Howard Ainslee."

"Howard, my brother, you don't mean to tell me he is here?"

"That's the identical chap, Frances, but it's his own secret. Several times I have been on the point of discovering him to himself, but I waiting for him to take the lead. He knows me, but he doesn't know that I know him."

At this juncture in the conversation they were interrupted by hearing a canoe come into the inlet and paddled directly towards their fire.

"Will it be Rheinhardt?" Mrs. MacGregor asked with startled voice. Her fears kept picturing to herself the approach of this man with every swaying of the underwood seen, or breaking of a limb heard.

Rory MacKenzie did not answer, but involuntarily he put one hand on his pistol and the other on his hunting knife, just to assure himself they were there in readiness if needed.

As soon as the canoe was beached and the occupant was disembarked, his profile quite visible from the light of their cheerful fire, Mrs. MacGregor rose up hurriedly and with an exclamation of surprised joy:

"It is Charlie. Oh, Charlie, my boy, it is you."

In a moment the mother and son were in each other's embrace.

With this momentary break in the conversation it was resumed by Mrs. MacGregor's announcement to her son:

"Major MacKenzie has just been telling me all about your father and his mine. How I wish you had been here that you might have heard it too."

Turning to Major MacKenzie, the boy asked him, "Do you think my father was killed, Major MacKenzie?"

"We haven't the least doubt about it Charlie." the Major answered, speaking familiarly to the boy, as if they were of long acquaintanceship.

"By the German trader, Rheinhardt?"

"It could be no one else." Major Mackenzie replied.

"Rheinhardt spread the story about that it was the Major here who was the murderer," his mother interjected.

Charlie looked up towards the Major, saying nothing, but waiting for his expected answer.

"The only difficulty about that was that I happened to be north at the time," the Major explained. "The money was saved, or a part of it, at least."

"Then my father didn't have his money with him?"

"Oh, yes, but Rusty Brown and two Indians got wind somehow that your father was being pursued by Rheinhardt. They reached there in time to save the money, but too late to save your father."

"Did they see Rheinhardt?"

"They saw a boat pull away from the island when they hove in sight, but they we too far from them to know whose it was. When they got to the island, your father's body was still warm."

"There were two Frenchies with him, I heard Captain Ike say."

"Yes, but their bodies were thrown into a crack of a rock, and covered over with stones. My man, Hank Bryant, got the whole story lately from one of his men, and when I accused him of it to-day, and told him the details, he looked the guilty man that he is. But to-morrow he'll forfeit his life for his crimes, or there's no justice in Heaven."

"This Rusty Brown is up here now." Charlie informed them.

"He is!" exclaimed the Major, with pleased surprise. "Then he'll be my backer to-morrow, when I send Rheinhardt across

You know Frances, he and I are to have a duel to-morrow."

"Oh, surely not, Major," exclaimed Mrs. MacGregor with unfeigned alarm.

"Yes, Hector and I have come from the north to put an end to him, or he to us. We have talked it over and we have both concluded it is time something was done. I had my gun ready to do it to-day, but we both fought side by side in the same army, and I felt the only honest way to finish him would be in a duel. Yes, he'll go across to-morrow, of this I am sure."

"I heard Lieutenant MacLeod saying he was going to have it out with Rheinhardt to-morrow," Charlie intercepted, emphasizing the pronoun so that Major MacKenzie might be informed that there was another who was contemplating the same task as himself.

"Well, if Hector MacLeod says he is going to do anything, then it's done. I'm glad he's made up his mind at last." Then turning to Mrs. MacGregor he continued, "You know Flora's mother made him promise he would not avenge Flora's death, and she would not let him go until he gave it to her.

I have been trying to persuade him ever since that if he persists in keeping that promise he is as bad as the Israelitish sovereign who made a fool of a vow, and, to keep it, murdered his daughter, teaching the whole world since that there are some vows which must be broken if we would do that which is God-appointed and right."

"And why didn't she want Hector to avenge the dishonourable conduct of a criminal against the one who was as dear to him as life itself?" asked Mrs. MacGregor with spirit, intermixed not a little with a venom of hate.

"I suppose," answered MacKenzie, "she wanted that honour for her son."

"And why didn't he do it?" asked Charlie.

"Couldn't," replied the Major quite solemnly. "He was killed in the war, you know."

"Then after her son and Lieutenant MacLeod, who was next of kin?"

"I suppose I am. You see I'm his first cousin. Our mothers were sisters, and first cousin also to Flora on my father's side. I told Hector when we set out this time that if he wouldn't, I must. Now I have three reasons why I must."

"Three!" exclaimed Mrs. MacGregor. "What are they, Major?"

"First, because Flora and I were sister and brother in friendship and cousins by blood; second, because he accused me of the crime of which himself was guilty; and third, because I have challenged him and he has accepted.

"If you had done that at first, Major MacKenzie, my father would be still living," interjected Charlie.

"Oh, Charlie, how can you say that?" his mother gently chided. She was afraid Major MacKenzie might resent the reproof which was couched in his statement.

But if Major MacKenzie observed any reproof, certainly he did not heed it. He, too, was considering when freedom from punishment is justifiable and when not.

"Perhaps so," he meditated abstractedly, "perhaps so. Yes, it is difficult at times to determine when wrong-doing should be treated with leniency and when not."

"I suppose I am next of kin to father," Charlie further interposed, as of one who felt himself a responsible partner in the task of eliminating a criminal from the community life of the La Cloche.

"Charlie, Charlie, don't think any more about that dreadful man. I do hope we may get out of here safely," said his mother.

But were she able to see she would have noticed a flush of excitement on the face of her son, as of one contemplating some great adventure.

"I Wish I were the shot Hector MacLeod is," he continued, paying no heed mother's admonition.

A trembling fear came into the m Mrs. MacGregor. "Can he be contemplating to avenge his father's death?" she thought, as she heard him express his wish to duplicate the other lad's successful exploit in the morning.

"Do you know what father's last words were, mother?" he asked.

"I do not suppose, my dear boy, any one will ever know that," she answered with a heavy heart.

"I know, mother. Hector MacLeod told me last night. 'For God's sake, Rheinhardt, think of my wife and little boy!' These were his last words and they have been ringing in my ears all day."

"Poor Claire, poor Claire," repeated his mother between her sobs.

It is woman's spirit to weep; but man was born, not to bemoan an ill-fate, but to triumph over it.

"Do you think Hector MacLeod would be afraid of Rheinhardt if he killed his father?" he asked, as if he were contemplating some task, and seeking inducements to encourage himself in its undertaking.

His mother was too absorbed in her sorrow, her wounded heart torn afresh by the messages she had received concerning her husband and his last surviving days, to realize the dangerous feat which he was contemplating. Not so Major MacKenzie. The youth had stumbled on an ugly truth, 'The avenger of blood shall be the next of kin.'

"He must know," thought MacKenzie, as he listened to him, "that the task is his, not ours."

Our destiny is assuredly not a matter of personal choice. Charlie found himself confronted with one of those mysterious problems of life, the meaning of which, willing or unwilling, circumstances decreed he must solve. Would justice lay its heavy hand upon his shoulder and demand of him, a youth yet in his teens, a service which required the resources of a strong, matured and courageous man, to rightly perform. This was the thought passing through the mind of Major MacKenzie.

"Yes, he is next of kin, but the lad is too young, his shoulders too weak to bear the weight of so great a burden." He therefore resolved in his mind that, in this instance, justice required that the task be performed vicariously.

"You are next of kin we know, Charlie, in respect to one of Rheinhardt's crime, but not to his first. MacLeod is next of kin there, and I am next to him. Justice must be done for the first blood before we strike a blow for the second. If we fail, Charlie, then it must be you."

"Oh, Major, how could you put a thought like that in the mind of the boy?" Mrs. MacGregor was not averse to having Rheinhardt punished, but she would rather see the murder unavenged than that her son should be the instrument in the hands of justice in its performance.

"Frances," Major MacKenzie spoke in a kindly, yet determined spirit, "the law is not ours, but God's. In His plan of the world there is no place for crime. When a man commits a crime, it is God he must face to answer for his crime, not man. It is God who decrees the law, but it is man who must put it into execution. To-morrow Oscar Rheinhardt must pay the penalty for his first crime. If he gets past, then I haven't known Hector MacLeod for fifty years. But if he gets past him, he'll not get past me. But if he gets past both of us"—and Major MacKenzie flouted the very thought of such a possibility, "then it is Charlie."

"In a battle, sometimes it happens when the first line fails, then the second line of support must step in. And sometimes, but not very often, even the third line. Never fear for the boy, Frances. Oscar Rheinhardt hasn't got past the first line yet, and I don't think he ever will."

At this juncture Major MacKenzie arose, as if preparations for the undertaking should be immediately made. "It is getting late and we must get back to the boys, for they'll be wondering what has happened to us."

CHAPTER XVIII

THE LAST DUEL

When the Indians got back to the trading-post after leaving Mrs. MacGregor in secluded isolation and captivity in a trapper's hut, they found that the shooting which disturbed them was occasioned by nothing more than the arrival of the flock of wild geese, the leader of which had been brought down so unexpectedly alongside of Hector.

"Where is the wumman?" enquired Rheinhardt.

"In trapper's hut at Fox Bluff," answered the leader.

"See anything of MacLeod?" he asked.

The Indians answered in the negative.

"One of my men saw him, but he has disappeared suddenly out of view," Rheinhardt continued. "Did he see you take her there?"

"Maybe, maybe not," answered the same Indian, the spokesman of the quartette, "how we know?"

The possibility of such an eventuality, voiced by the Indian, added to the perturbed state of Rheinhardt's mind, who was still chafing over the unsatisfactory ending of their morning's proceedings. What then must have been his surprise, when turning around, he observed Rory MacKenzie standing by listening to every word spoken. MacKenzie did not wait for any salutation.

"Rheinhardt," he began with a slow and measured voice, "what have you done with Mrs. MacGregor?"

"That's my business, not yours, MacKenzie."

"With that MacKenzie leaped at Rheinhardt, pushed the muzzle of his rifle against his abdomen, and forced him to stand, backing against a tree.

"Rheinhardt, if you had your deserts, I would shoot you dead this very minute. What have you done with Mrs. MacGregor?"

The Hessian, now cowed and irresolute, and knowing full well the ability of MacKenzie to carry out his threat, answered. "Just where the Indians left her. If you want her, you can have her."

"Rheinhardt, the score between us must be settled to-day. Shall it be a duel, or shall I finish you now? We have both been soldiers. You, a German and American; I, a British and Canadian one. You have come now to the end of your tether. Shall it be a duel or shall I finish you now?" MacKenzie repeated.

Rheinhardt seeing that he must accept one of two evils, neither of which he would choose if he could escape them, accepted the duel as the lesser of the two.

"A duel, if you want it, I'm ready to meet you," he answered, having gained somewhat his composure and a measure of his usual bravado.

"You are the Hessian who was shot by Mrs. MacLean at The Beeches, aren't you?"

"No, I'm not, answered Rheinhardt unabashedly.

"You're not? Part his whiskers there, boys," MacKenzie ordered, while he kept the riffle-muzzle pressing close against his person.

Hank Bryant, who had been keeping Rheinhardt under observation, and wan immediately at hand when the altercation between the two started, stepped up and did as his master commanded, disclosing the bullet wound first on the one cheek, and then on the other. This evidence of his identity was conclusive.

"Oscar Rheinhardt, up to this you have escaped justice and you have added crime to crime, but the end of this career of crime has come. There is one here now who bears the name of MacLeod. There's another who bears the name of MacGregor. Together they have come here accompanied by the spirits of the departed. To them belongs, first, the right and duty; and if they fail, then there are twenty others, who have made a vow that the law of justice shall not miscarry, and among that twenty I shall be the first. This house, which you meant as a prison for Mrs. MacGregor, shall become your own, and this place which you meant for crime, shall become a house of justice.

Rheinhardt now at bay, assured him that he would fight them all, one after another in any order they would name.

"To-morrow, then let it be," accepted MacKenzie forthwith. "And where?" It was the custom of the region that the one challenged should be given the naming of the place where the combat should be staged.

Deliberating for a time, partly to gain his wind, and partly in an effort to think out some way of escape, Rheinhardt answered after considerable pause, "Beaver Lake."

"Beaver Lake! Then let it be. You have three chances, Rheinhardt, and to-morrow you must take them all."

Turning to the two men, Conossoway and Bryant, he gave command as an officer of an army, accustomed to be obeyed, that they should keep such guard as to make his escape impossible.

The arrangement of the duel completed Rheinhardt began to ponder seriously the dilemma set before him. One chance against three in his favour. 'Would he win out? Every time hitherto he had been able to cheat the Avenger of Blood out of his expectations. Would to-morrow bring him his usual luck?

A close student of human nature, if he had followed the ways of Rheinhardt, could not but know that this man was already being tracked down by the Avenger of Blood. The bleared eye, the bloated cheek, the descending scale in the standard of manhood which he exemplified, told patently that in the region of manhood, the inner and nobler life, this man was already dead. The killing of the body could not add anything to or take anything away from the complete punishment which had been meted out to him there. But justice has its own ways of dealing with those who disregard its laws, and the death of the body, as an exemplification to those who esteem lightly its laws, is oftentimes made to befit the crime.

The sun rose clear and bright over the peak of the La Cloche, on the morning of the day appointed for the duel. The camp of Lieutenant MacLeod was early astir. Rusty Brown and the three boys with Major MacKenzie were already on their way to Beaver Lake. Mrs. MacGregor was still at the Wigwam and under the care of the Indian family who had brought about her release.

Little Knife and Conossoway had their canoe embarked and were waiting for MacLeod to accompany them to the place appointed for the duel. The two boys were seated at the table with a steaming roast of venison and vegetable diet before them. Louis Conossoway was standing at the door with a rifle in his hand. Lieutenant MacLeod at the far end was giving his final instructions to them before his departure.

"Can you shoot, Charlie?"

"Yes, was the answer of the lad, "but not as good as Hector."

"Then keep your wits about you to-day, lads. Louis, you'll stalk the woods between here and the Sault du Nouailles, and see that Rheinhardt passes before you to the Beaver Lake. If you see him seeking to escape, you must shoot and kill."

Turning to Charlie, he said, "He has murdered your father. We know now he has, and to-day he must answer before God for his crime. 'The Avenger of Blood shall be the next of kin.' You Charlie, are next of kin to Claire MacGregor, and I am next of kin to Flora. On us God has laid this work."

Turning to Hector, he continued, but in a more subdued tone and spirit, "You, Hector, are next of kin to me, I would to God that I could, but if I cannot, then you, I pass it on to you, my next of kin. Louis will place you where I instructed. Rising to depart he shook hands first with Charlie, then Hector. Holding his nephew's hand in affectionate clasp, he spake some words in the Gaelic, which interpreted, meant, "The Blessing of God upon you, lad, and your family."

With this he passed out of the room quickly, and took his place in the middle of the canoe, with the two Indian companions.

Immediately after, the three boys struck out in another canoe going by way of the Sault du Nouailles as they were instructed. When they reached the foot of the gorge, they disembarked and travelled overland the rest of the way. They followed the bank of the river, originally the highway of the wild animals of this region, but now the trail the woodsman, hunter and explorer.

"This trail will take us to Beaver Lake," the young Indian informed them.

Louis had often travelled this route before, and knew every turn to take to bring them to the place which they had set out to reach. It led them through a greatly diversified but always rough territory. Now it was a narrow gorge between the walls of high, precipitous rocks through which they were passing; then they emerged from this to find before them a clay highland, through which in the course of persistent years, the river had cut its channel. The outcroppings of rock were found all along on their path, which they had to either circle around or climb over.

As they approached near their goal, the trail left the bank of the river, and took to the heights some distance from the shore. Louis led on, setting a pace easily followed up by the two boys. The cool, crisp October air, added to their physical fitness and supplied them with the needed energy for the day's exertions. They followed this eminence, not too closely covered with trees, and that mainly poplar and birch, until they came to a place where it dropped in quick descent to a large valley below. Here they halted to survey their surroundings.

Louis climbed up on a large rock boulder and bade the two boys to come up to his side. What a sight before their view! Below them was a large meadow where the stream meandered, now very slowly in its widened channel, a channel known to the natives by the name of Beaver Lake. Save where the stream passed through, the meadow was hedged in on all sides by clumps of black alders, set so closely together that it was hardly possible for a passage to be made through them. Behind these alders, the pine and spruce and tamarack formed a deep wooded thicket, the foreground of the forest behind, and the background of the black alders immediately surrounding the meadow. The forest stretched for miles round about, covering the La Cloche hills with a variety of colour that gave ample evidence of the season of the year. The dark red of the sumach, the scarlet of the maple, the yellow of the silver-birch, and the purple of the wild-cherry, were mingled in pleasing harmony with the deep green of the more favoured trees which had as yet resisted the encroachment of the autumn weather on their life.

This was the most beautiful landscape that Hector had ever viewed, more beautiful by far than anything on Parry Island, or any other of the beautiful islands of the lake. For miles this panorama of beauty stretched itself before them, gradually being lifted up skyward, until it reached its highest eminence in the rounded head of a gray rock, one of the highest peaks of the La Cloche mountains. Above this peak the sun shone down clear and bright from an unclouded sky, revealing to them every detail of the scenery.

On the far side of the meadow, a. herd of deer were grazing leisurely wholly oblivious of the fact that near them were gathering together groups of men armed with deadly rifles. At the far edge of the alder thicket, a stag stood with its head resting on the shoulders of a doe, while near them a couple of fawn were playing. To the right of them the rock rose up in conical shape, at the foot of which and forming the bank of the river, was an open space, a sand beach, the place appointed for the fatal duel.

On this beach, the boys observed the two groups of men who formed the parties to the duel, gathered. At the farther side were Rheinhardt's men, while MacLeod, MacKenzie, Rusty Brown and several others stood at the near end. Louis Conossoway selected a spot as he was instructed at a place about a hundred yards distant from where Rheinhardt with his men were standing. With his rifle in his hand, behind a rock boulder and a clear line between him and the Hessian, Hector took his place unobserved.

At the time appointed Rheinhardt and MacLeod, each with his rifle in his hand, was stepping into his place. Hector placed his rifle in readiness and watched with lynx-like alertness every movement of Rheinhardt.

"Are you timid," asked Louis of him.

"No, I am not," he answered back with fearless courage.

Lieutenant MacLeod was thinking not of the present, but of the past. Before him, in vision, stood a demented woman wrestling from him an unwilling assent, "Promise me you'll not add crime to crime, but leave it to God." But Rheinhardt was alive to the situation.

Cruel and criminal by nature and habit he awaited not the signal which the duel code demanded, but drew up his weapon and fired before MacLeod had reached his place. In a trice, the whole valley was full of frightened life. The many cries of the wildfowl rose up in unison, proclaiming in excited tones, that some catastrophe had befallen their unsuspecting valley, some enemy had intruded upon their peaceful domain. The quacks of the wild duck, as they rose in flocks from amongst the weeds along the shallow waters on the shore of the lake, were mingled with the squawk of a water-hen as it flew to some more sheltering place among the bulrushes of the meadow. A huge crane rose up and started off in sudden flight to a neighbouring lake to escape the danger it deemed impending. The deer all bounded in rapid flight to the one spot where entered their runway into the meadow, and with them the stag and doe, nor looked behind to see whether their fawn were following.

Just then something else and unexpected happened. Hardly had the echo of Rheinhardt's fatal shot reached the hillside when the criminal fell backward, a crumpled heap upon the ground. Pierced from ear to ear, the bullet of the next-of-kin had reached its intended destination, and the spirit of the criminal went forth to take up its abode in its own befitting region. As his whole life, so was his last act, a crime against law and order and life.

Rusty Brown rushed immediately to the boulder from whence the report of the third shot proceeded and questioned in excited tones, "Hector MacLeod, was it you? Was it you?"

The nephew stood cool and calm, save a. little red flush on each cheek.

"I saw my uncle fall, and as I was next-of kin, I shot to kill and I feel that I did my duty."

"To-day," repeated the brother of Mrs. MacGregor, "the Scriptures have been fulfilled. Blood for blood, and the avenger of Hector Campbell MacLeod had to be next of kin."

When Hector Campbell MacLeod fell the two Indian companions of his forest life rushed to his side, and, lifting up his bleeding form, bore it away into the woods. Among hills of La Cloche they laid it down to rest, peaceably and undisturbedly in its last long sleep, side by side with his Flora.

Major MacKenzie ran to the spot where Rheinhardt fell, and when he observed the bullet wound, remarked in solemn and satisfied assurance, "He is dead; yes, dead."

When he had satisfied himself that there was no miscarriage of justice, he hastened to the other end of the line, but there was no MacLeod there. With as quick despatch as the body of Tecumseh from the battlefield on the Thames, so disappeared the body of the soldier, trader and explorer, from the fatal spot where he had fallen on the shingly shore of Beaver Lake. In the warfare of life, the fates had played against him an unfair game and this last event was but in keeping with the rest. But there is a legend among the Ottawas, that, though his body lieth peaceably and undisturbedly at rest in its last long sleep by the side of his Flora, yet on the night of that tragic day, two spirits were seen to wend their way together to the heavenly heights, for, those whom God hath joined together the prince of dark angels cannot muster sufficient power to wrest asunder.

Thus closed with tragic import from the last duel fought on the bay. In the early morning of the second day after, the four boys of the Parry Island camp embarked on Captain Ike's schooner to sail southward, gladdened in heart that, notwithstanding their fears for two long weeks, there was to be no break in their ranks as they made the return journey homeward. Hector took affectionate farewell of Rusty Brown and Charlie.

"I knew we would find you," were the words of Rusty, as with tear-filled eyes, he shook hands heartily with him. "The ship was right side up in the fire; it never fails."

As the ship moved out they saw Major MacKenzie and Mrs. MacGregor standing side by side waving them adieu, and Charlie looking wistfully in their direction as if he would fain wish that he, too, were one of their number.

This brings to a close the record of an historic past, a page of which has been opened and read to us, that we might cherish anew the memories of these forerunners of our present and better civilization. Progress and achievement, education and religion, followed each other after this in close succession, and the coarser and criminal sides of life had to give place to the reign of law and order. The old order perished but the new advanceth to a nobler and higher future.

FINIS

ABOUT THE AUTHOR

Rev. Hugh Cowan (May 20, 1867 – April 19, 1943) was a Presbyterian Church of Canada and later United Church of Canada minister, author, editor and historian.

Hugh Cowan was born on May 20, 1867 in Bentinck, Ontario, Canada to John Cowan and Mary McLean both of whom were born in Scotland.

John and Mary McLean Cowan

In 1893, he finished his Bachelor of Arts degree in Manitoba College. He pursued his Master of Arts at Knox College, Toronto in 1896. He later pursued his Bachelor of Divinity degree at Kingston, Ontario's Queen's Theological College and graduated in 1905.

During Cowan's first ministry at Rutherford Presbyterian Church in Dawn-Euphemia near Chatham, Ontario, he met Jean Eloise Wood who lived at nearby Langbank. They were married on October 31, 1899 in London, Ontario.

Hugh Cowan and Jean Eloise Wood had three daughters and six sons. James Alexander Cowan, Marjorie Jean Cowan Jolliffe, John Kenneth Cowan, Hugh Raymond Cowan, Mary Elizabeth Cowan, Grace Edith Cowan Fitzpatrick, Stuart McLean Cowan, Donald Murray Cowan and Alan Wood Cowan

Hugh and Jean Cowan

Church ministry

Cowan was ordained by the Chatham Presbytery of the Presbyterian Church of Canada in August 17, 1897.

Cowan served as a pastor in Oakdale United Church (formerly known as Oakdale Presbyterian Church), and Rutherford Presbyterian Church in Lambton County from 1897 to 1900, in St. Andrew's Presbyterian Church in North Easthope and Shakespeare Presbyterian Church in Shakespeare, Perth County, Ontario from 1900 to 1905, a minister in charge of St. Paul's Presbyterian Church in Harwich Township, Kent County, Ontario, Bethel Presbyterian Church, and The Ridge Presbyterian Church from 1905 to 1913, in Haynes Ave. Church in St. Catharines from 1914 to 1916, Chalmer's Presbyterian Church in Toronto from 1919 to 1921, and in High Park Presbyterian Church in 1922.

From 1925 to 1937, in various congregations of the United Church of Canada, he served as a minister at Bethel United Church near Chatham, Ontario, as a pastor at MacLennan, Desbarats and Port Rock near Sault Ste. Marie, and Sault Suburban Church area charge in Sault Ste. Marie.

Cowan has authored numerous historical books. One was *Canadian Achievement in the Province of Ontario – The Detroit River District* where he wrote about the history of the Canadian people in Detroit River area including Essex county and Windsor, Ontario. The book was recently republished as Ontario and the Detroit Frontier 1701-1814. A similar unpublished work on the history of Chatham and Kent County was also written. He created *Gold and Silver Jubilee, Sault Ste. Marie, Canada* detailing

more the history of Sault Ste. Marie. A monthly publication Mer Douce was produced for three years and is one of the important historical references for the Manitoulin Island, Georgian Bay and Muskoka areas.

He also wrote a fictional book entitled *La Cloche. The Story of Hector MacLeod and His Misadventures in the Georgian Bay and the La Cloche Districts* which is an adventure tale.

Jean and Hugh Cowan

Cowan also published this book centering on the progress of Christianity called *The Great Drama of Human Life*.

Cowan served as the managing editor of Algonquin Historical Society of Canada.

He retired in 1937.

Hugh Cowan's Wikipedia article is at http://en.wikipedia.org/wiki/Hugh_Cowan

Hugh Cowan died at the General and Marine Hospital in Owen Sound, Ontario on April 19, 1943 at the age of 73.

SILVERWOODS PUBLISHING BOOKS

BOOKS TO DISCOVER

Learning to See =
Seeing to Learn

Vision, Learning & Behavior in Children

Dr. Patrick T. Quaid

NEW HOPE
FOR
CONCUSSIONS TBI & PTSD

BY
DR. LAWRENCE D. KOMER
JOAN CHANDLER KOMER

Foreword by Jack Canfield
Co-Creator of the New York Times #1 best-selling
series Chicken Soup for the Soul®

BE GREAT.
RISE AND CONQUER

BRUCE COLERO

TWO:
One Destined to Addiction
the Other to be Free

Alexander T. Polgar Ph.D.

Conducting
Parenting
Capacity
Assessments

A Manual for
Mental Health
Practitioners

Alexander T. Polgar

Beyond Addiction:
Sally Discovers How
To Think For Herself

ALEXANDER T. POLGAR Ph.D.

FINDING PURPOSE
AND MEANING:
Sally Survives Her Brief,
Nasty Dance With Psychiatry

ALEXANDER T. POLGAR Ph.D.

FREEDOM:
SALLY GETS SOBER
AND STARTS TO
GROW UP

ALEXANDER T. POLGAR Ph.D.

Because we can - we must

Achieving the
Human Developmental
Potential

In Five Generations

Alexander T. Polgar Ph.D.

Silverwoods
Publishing